Maiden Manoeuvres

Volume 1 of The Sisters' Saga

Alison Ferguson

Backstory Press

Cover: Scott Mair

Email: backstorypress@gmail.com

Website: backstorypress.com

For Ian

Contents

Chapter 1

Time you behaved like a young lady

Henrietta twisted the hank of her horse's mane about her fingers. Casting a glance behind her, she saw to her satisfaction that her cousins trailed far behind. She glimpsed them through the trees in the distance, where Jack and Bert waited for Eliza to catch up. Eliza might be her favourite cousin and dearest friend, but she rode too slowly to stay alongside. Once her brothers returned, then she could ride as fast as she liked.

Her horse settled back to his natural stride, giving Henrietta a chance to take in the scene about her. In the four long years since Papa left the colony to go back to England, all the things he'd planned had been done: the saltpans had been established; the saltworks were up and running; the building of the limeworks was near completion; and the paddocks were finally fenced. He'd be pleased; she was sure of it. Mama said he might even get back today if his ship wasn't delayed by the weather. Once he was back, Mama wouldn't have so much to do with the estate and so she wouldn't keep snapping that it was Henrietta's responsibility to keep an eye on her sisters.

Distractions had been few since Mrs Oakes disgraced herself by getting married to Mr Ridgeway.

Whenever possible, Henrietta slipped down to the salt-maker's house to visit her. But when rain cooped her inside, she played her pianoforte. She was working on a sonata by Haydn at the moment in preparation for Papa's return. The dynamics of the second movement troubled her; Papa would be sure to notice if she got it wrong.

Thudding hooves heralded her cousins catching up.

'Beat you back to the stables,' shouted Jack as he raced his horse past hers.

'Come on, Henrietta, don't be a slow coach,' called Bert as he passed.

Exasperated, she kicked her heels back into the horse's flanks and joined the race. Her hair whipped loose from her plait as she sped with the wind behind her. Panting and laughing, she arrived at the same moment as Jack at the stump that marked their unofficial finish line.

'Beat you,' he said.

'Did not.'

'Did too. Didn't I, Bert?'

'I don't know. I was behind both of you.'

They argued until Eliza joined them, and then they all walked the horses back towards the stables. Henrietta was arrested by the sight of her mother standing on the verandah stock-still, her face rigid with anger. Her mother lifted a finger to beckon her.

'Good luck,' Eliza muttered.

Her mother waited until Henrietta reached the verandah before she turned and strode to the drawing room. Now Henrietta knew she was in very great trouble indeed.

'Bareback, again. Have you no regard for your personal safety to be so reckless? What would your father say?'

Eliza gave Henrietta a rueful smile from where she hovered by the doorway.

'But the boys—' Henrietta started.

Her mother ploughed ahead. 'And seated astride. No sense of decorum. At thirteen, it's high time you behaved like a young lady. Your father's return is imminent, and what sort of woman will he find you are growing into?'

'But it's hard to sit side-saddle if you're riding bareback,' Henrietta said in a rush. She then forced herself to slow to a reasonable tone. 'And so it's safer, and so I'm not being—'

'Your cousin Eliza is content to ride side-saddle. She doesn't need to show off.'

Henrietta tried to appear chastened.

'You can be grateful your uncle and aunt will be back with their guest any minute, otherwise you'd be hearing a lot more about this. As it is, well, I can only be thankful they weren't here to witness you disgrace your family.' She stalked back into the hallway, adding over her shoulder, 'Mind you tidy yourself up before they arrive.'

Struggling with silent giggles, Henrietta and Eliza followed in her wake.

At the far end of the hall, silhouetted by the blaze of the day outside, her uncle and aunt walked through the door. A short, round man waddled along behind them.

'We are the bearers of good news,' Uncle Herbert said, tossing his hat into the air.

The stranger's plump face was red, and he was puffing from exertion.

Henrietta ducked behind her mother and smoothed her loose strands of hair back into her plait. Straightening, she clasped her hands in front of her demurely.

Uncle Herbert waved a hand towards the red-faced man. 'May I present Mr Alfred Babcock—the poor man's been suffering from heat exhaustion ever since we left the harbour-side. They don't have this kind of weather in Massachusetts in autumn, he tells me.'

Henrietta's mother smiled but her eyes remained fixed on her brother-in-law.

Mr Babcock gave a low bow. For a moment, he teetered as though about to topple forward. 'Delighted to make your acquaintance, Mrs Burbridge,' he said in an American accent. His tight cravat pushed up the folds of flesh about his neck. 'And this must be?'

'Our eldest daughter, Henrietta.' Her mother moved aside.

The shield of her mother's back gone, Henrietta dropped her gaze. She avoided looking at Eliza in case she laughed outright.

'But Herbert, the news?' her mother asked.

Uncle Herbert beamed, and Aunt Elizabeth caught her sister-in-law up a hug. 'Finally, you'll have them all home again. Their carriage is right behind us.'

Henrietta didn't wait for the adults. She raced along the hall and down the steps. In a haze of dust, the second carriage rattled up the drive. Henrietta took a deep breath to compose herself. She'd show her father she'd grown into the *young lady* her mother wanted her to be. As the carriage drew up, hands waved out the windows. Her brothers' heads popped out, and she abandoned her composure. Shrieking, she ran to them.

Bill, now taller than her, shook her hand as if they were adults, but spoiled the charade by blushing with excitement. Griffith kept talking so fast she could barely understand him.

She turned to greet her father only to find he had gone into the house.

'It's only going to be the family,' her mother admonished as Henrietta skittered from room to room several days later.

Henrietta laid out the dress she planned to wear. She practised the pianoforte piece she would perform for her father after dinner. She rushed through the chores her mother set her and practised some more.

'Nothing to be so excited about,' said her mother.

But Henrietta could tell that her mother felt just as buoyant; the brisk clip of her mother's shoes tapped up and down the hall as she directed the preparations.

Cook's shouts at Ann, the newly assigned servant, that she was a lazy good-for-nothing, punctuated the day. Mary and Susan polished silver until their hands were grimy. The big oak table in the dining room was cranked open to add two more leaves, so they could seat twelve.

With nothing left for her to do, Henrietta longed to get outside and ride with her brothers, but Mama had imprisoned her as punishment for riding bareback.

Henrietta had caught only the occasional glimpse of her father since his return. Each time his face had been set in a stern frown as he left the house to ride into Parramatta for meetings with Governor Macquarie or into Sydney Town, sorting out business.

She couldn't understand the reasons for his sourness. Tonight, they would celebrate his return. Tonight, he'd be cheerful and pay attention to her like he used to, considering each word she said. Four years ago, she'd been a child—the same age as her nine-year-old sister Beth was now. Beth was nice enough, but it wasn't as if what she said was interesting. Papa might have been humouring Henrietta back then. Now that she was thirteen and, as her mother so often reminded her, nearly grown-up, her conversation would be really of interest.

In the flickering candlelight, faces hid their thoughts. The adults sat towards one end, grouped about her father at the head of the table, her mother on his right, with Aunt Elizabeth on his left staring studiously at her plate. Uncle Herbert's cheery smile had faded. The adults talked only sporadically, eating slowly.

Their sombre mood leaked across the dining table to where the older children from the two brothers' families sat. Her two brothers, Bill and Griffith, flanked her, facing their cousins. Her eleven-year-old sister, Rose, perched there too—too young to remain with the adults on such an occasion, in Henrietta's opinion—but she had been allowed to join them to make an even twelve. Too cowed by formality to speak, Rose sat wide-eyed, her mouth open. *If she's not careful, she'll catch a fly,* thought Henrietta, before realising that a thick silence now lay heavily between the adults.

Aunt Elizabeth broke the impasse, saying, 'This might be a matter best talked about another time?

Away from the table.' She nodded towards the children.

Four years in England had left Mr William Burbridge with a pasty pallor that now greyed as he said through gritted teeth, 'It has to be said, so I'm saying it now. Things have not been managed well while I've been away.' His glare swung between his wife and his brother. 'Governor Macquarie has taken advantage of my absence to misdirect you as to the family's obligations. Herbert, you should have known better.'

Uncle Herbert flushed, his tanned face deepening to mahogany.

Aunt Elizabeth rose with effort, weighted by her confinement, now well advanced. 'My apologies, gentlemen, please excuse me. I'm afraid I must seek a more comfortable seat in the drawing room.'

The two men half-rose as the women and children left. To Henrietta, following her aunt across the hall, the distance bridged one world and another.

Aunt Elizabeth eased herself onto the chaise lounge, and Henrietta's mother sat nearby. The chime from the clock marked the hour. A quick knock and the door burst open. Henrietta's youngest sister, Elizabeth Maria, rushed in, and behind her toddled their youngest cousin, Charles.

Susan hurried in after the children. 'Sorry, Mrs Burbridge, Mrs Burbridge,' she said to each of the women, 'but I couldn't hold them back any longer, they were that excited.' Her bob of a curtsy was hampered by baby cousin Margaret perched on her hip.

The hubbub from the children lit the room as brightly as the lamps.

Bill picked up the deck of cards and began to shuffle. 'Faro, anyone? Jack and me against Griffith and Bert,' he said.

Griffith looked to Henrietta to be his partner. She played cards better than her cousins, and Griffith had lost all his pocket money to his brother during their return voyage with their father.

But Henrietta shook her head and said, 'Come on, Eliza, let's play with the babies.'

Eliza's mouth opened in mock shock. Such a suggestion usually came from her, not Henrietta.

Henrietta ignored her. She wanted to hear what her mother and Aunt Elizabeth might say about the argument at dinner, and she knew the younger children would stay in the vicinity of their mothers.

From the sound of the loud voices across the hall, the dispute continued between her father and Uncle Herbert. She glanced over to the pianoforte and wondered if she might still get to perform her piece later. Tears prickled, and she blinked them back, furious at herself for being such a child.

Grabbing Bessie, her old rag doll, from the basket of toys which Susan brought in, Henrietta dangled it along the floor to lure Charles to join her.

Eliza shrugged then lifted baby Margaret from Susan's arms. She sat cross-legged on the rug beside Henrietta. 'Do you think Mr Babcock will be at the wedding?' she whispered. 'I think he's taken a shine to you.'

Henrietta frowned, trying to listen to her mother and aunt.

'He's not going to let the matter go, you know,' her mother said. 'He never lets anything drop.'

Eliza tried again. 'Will your mother let you wear your new muslin dress?'

Henrietta didn't answer.

Aunt Elizabeth sniffed. 'Well, you know the Burbridges. Robbed of their lands on the Isle of Thanet by William the Conqueror, and it still rankles.' She swung her feet up on to the seat.

From her position on the floor, Henrietta could see Aunt Elizabeth's ankles were red and swollen.

'At this rate,' continued her aunt, rubbing her belly, 'I might not make Miss Carter's wedding, though that might be a blessing. I'm not sure I can face the pews at St John's.'

Little Charles tossed Bessie under the settee in disgust. Henrietta stretched out on her stomach, reaching across the rug to retrieve the doll.

'I don't see what else I could have done,' Henrietta's mother said. 'What Governor Macquarie proposed made sense at the time. He is the governor, after all.'

'Mama,' said Eliza. 'It won't be too cold, will it? Henrietta and I want to wear our new dresses to the wedding. We can, can't we?'

Eliza's mother ignored the distraction. 'You know you did the right thing. Herbert said so.' Aunt Elizabeth paused as if uncertain whether to go on. 'And William wasn't here, was he?' She then went on. 'And even if he had been here, no doubt he would have made the same decisions.'

Charles made a grab for Bessie, tugging the doll from Henrietta's grip. Bessie's arm ripped as Henrietta jerked her away from him. Instantly, Charles set up a wail.

'Henrietta, whatever are you doing to your cousin?' her mother snapped. But the sound of the men's boots in the hall brought her up short.

The door opened, and the cold air came in with it.

Chapter 2

A refuge from sin

St John's Church had been erected in the way of all English churches, defying light and air to seep through its long window slits. Encased in her woollen serge petticoat, Henrietta's thighs stuck together with a slick clamminess, and her tailbone ground against the pew. Her stomach churned. Could it be that scrap of sausage she'd snatched from Rose's plate, left abandoned in the morning sun? She wriggled and fanned the pages of her hymnbook.

Her mother, tall and erect on her right, frowned. On the other side of her mother, her father didn't turn, but Henrietta saw the flicker of the muscles in his cheek.

She tried to bring her attention back to Reverend Marsden as he droned on.

'And the state of marriage is a blessing bestowed upon us by God and a ...'

In front of her sat Mr Babcock. His complexion mottled in the heat, so his whole face became pomegranate-red except for his upper lip, which remained a pallid white, beaded with sweat.

Her belly cramped, low and slow. She eased her shoulder blades to escape the cling of her dress against her back. Her mother's eyes flicked towards her in irritation.

'Marriage provides a refuge from sin and ...'

The light glanced off the bright brass buttons of the groom's guard of honour. The soldiers stood so straight in their smart red coats, every single one of them cast a handsome allure.

'For the creation of family and ...'

Eliza sat on the other side of the aisle, squashed next to old Mrs James and looking none too happy about it. Mrs James had come out to the colony with Uncle Herbert, ostensibly to help Aunt Elizabeth with the children. However, given her habit of dropping off to sleep the moment she sat down, her usefulness manifested only when standing.

The two Burbridge families hadn't seen each other since the disastrous dinner after her father's return. Griffith kept saying their father and Uncle Herbert would be sure to make up soon because, after all, they were brothers. She wasn't so sure and, even if they did, she couldn't imagine how it would be the same.

Her gaze returned to the row of soldiers, and she realised they all weren't as good-looking as on first sight. One had a spotty nose, another a sty in his eye, and another's shoulders were lopsided. But that one, the one she could see in profile, now he was remarkable. There was an illustration of Apollo at home in their book on Greek legends and here he was, in the flesh. His hair was dark, glossy and thick. His chin could have been chiselled from stone.

'And it is only right that a woman, being of weaker mind and disposition, obey her husband in all things ...'

Bill and Griffith were sitting in the pew behind her. Bill's foot jarred the back of her bench with irritating regularity. *Why are boys so annoying and yet men so ... alluring?* Henrietta cricked her head under the guise of adjusting her collar and caught Eliza's eye. She nodded in the direction of the handsome soldier. Eliza grinned back.

Rose and Beth stared at the Reverend Marsden with expressions that might have been rapt concentration. This was the first wedding they'd attended. Knowing their obsession, it was more likely to be the ornate flower arrangement behind the Reverend that had captured their attention.

The congregation rose with a rustle, hymnbooks in hand. Henrietta scrambled to join them.

Beth whispered, 'Which one?'

'The one nearest the pillar,' Henrietta said, her mind still on the soldier.

'Number, which number?' Beth said, riffling through the hymnbook. 'Which one are we singing?'

Henrietta hiccoughed in the effort not to giggle.

Her father leaned forward in front of her mother. 'Do you want me to take you outside, young lady?'

Henrietta flushed. She joined in the chorus, sharing her hymnbook with Beth.

After the last refrain, she sat back down and stayed resolutely stiff through the final prayers and church notices. She felt wretched. She didn't know why she was so miserable. Perhaps it was the thought that the handsome soldier might have witnessed her disgrace. Papa was so unfair; one minute expecting her to be a lady and then treating her like a child the next. She dabbed at her eyes with her handkerchief, just wiping the perspiration away, that was all.

Rising with the congregation, she turned to watch the bride and groom walk down the aisle towards the door.

'Henrietta,' Beth piped up. 'Did you sit on something?'

Henrietta twisted around. Rust coloured spots marked the back of her dress. She checked the pew: nothing. She couldn't think how the marks came to be there. Hands behind her back, she bunched the fabric together. If she could hide the stains, she could get Susan to clean it before her mother noticed.

'What's the problem?' Her mother pulled her about. A quiet hiss escaped through her teeth. 'Never mind, ma cherie.' She drew Henrietta closer with a light pat on her shoulder and manoeuvred the two of them so that her own dress obscured the view of Henrietta's skirts as they walked out.

Chapter 3

Apollo

Henrietta stifled a yawn while Griffith shuffled the cards. 'Come on, Griff, we're waiting.'

'Scuse me, Miss Burbridge,' Betty said, barging in after a notional knock on the door, 'but dinner's over and your muvver wants you in the drawing room wiv the guests.'

Henrietta shrugged. 'Sorry, Griff. I'll beat you another time.' She was out the door before he could object.

In the drawing room she found only her mother and her guest, Mrs Nairne, an old school friend.

'The governor's wife takes a great interest in her husband's business, doesn't she?' Mrs Nairne's lips curled in disapproval of such unseemly behaviour.

Henrietta caught a twinkle in her mother's eye.

'*Entre nous*, I overheard our Surgeon Superintendent talking on that very subject.' Her mother leaned forward. 'He was saying that Mrs Macquarie would really much rather be the governor than the goverwife.'

Mrs Nairne tittered behind her hand, then quickly assumed a mask of decorum. 'And here's your namesake—exactly like you were at the same age, so tall and graceful,' she said. 'Your mother had many suitors, Henrietta, all of them handsome. Your father was a lucky man. Still, not as many suitors available in New South Wales, I should think.'

'Now don't you be filling Henrietta's head with such notions. I'm sure we didn't think about such things at her age.'

'But Mr Babcock seems ...?'

Henrietta caught a coded glance between the two women.

'Well, time brings all things, I suppose,' Mrs Nairne muttered. She went on in a louder voice. 'Who would have imagined all those years ago at school we'd end up here on the other side of the world, so many miles from England?'

'As long as we count the miles, not the years.' Mrs Burbridge smiled.

'I confess I was quite jealous of your exotic parents,' Mrs Nairne said. 'Your French father, a Count, no less. And your mother, journeying all the way to India when she was but five years old. And then to become such a favourite of the governor-general.'

Henrietta was in no mood today for her mother's stories. She shifted restlessly. The card game upstairs would be well underway, she knew. Without her there, Griffith would win the pot. Her sisters were easy prey.

'My mother could not help become even more of a favourite of the Hastings as she grew,' continued Mrs Burbridge, 'for she was young and interesting with a mind of singular brightness and grace in *repartée*. How could a young lady with such *jeu d'ésprit* fail to attract nobility?'

Jeu d'ésprit—Henrietta turned the phrase over, relishing the words. She pictured herself attired in silk, being swept about a grand ballroom, laughing gaily at the words murmured in her ear. The figure of the gentleman remained ill-defined.

'Well, the Lord moves in mysterious ways,' said Mrs Nairne. 'I little thought when I used to listen to your stories about your life in India as a child that I'd end up travelling there myself. But I'm sure He has a plan, that's all I can say.'

Henrietta eyed the pianoforte with longing. Perhaps, her mother would ask her to play a piece. She saw her gloved fingers caress the keys while the same figure—still shadowy— turned the pages of her sheet music.

'You'll enjoy India, I'm sure,' said Mrs Burbridge. 'Mind you, the heat is insufferable and the smells are—'

'Smells?' came the hearty voice of Captain Nairne. 'It appears our decision to rejoin the ladies has been premature, gentlemen. Who knew our women-folk talked about such matters in our absence?'

He was followed into the room by her father and Mr Babcock.

Henrietta tensed as Mr Babcock pulled up the chair nearest to her, and said, 'Miss Burbridge, I'm so pleased your mother allowed you to join us. We were sorry not to have your company at dinner.' His American drawl extended the duration of his platitudes. Politeness spent, he turned back to the men. 'If we're talking about smells, Captain Nairne, you should come and see my haul from my latest whaling mission. Though, now I come to think of it, those seal skins *The Kinsmen* brought back last month smelled worse than Dead Horse Gully.'

Captain Nairne, perhaps regretting his opening sally, tried to steer the conversation towards more suitable matters. '*The Kinsmen*—Mr Burbridge, am I right in thinking that the ship is a joint enterprise for you and your brother?'

In the silence that followed, Henrietta became aware of the ticking from the clock in the hall. The rift between her father and Uncle Herbert had occurred over two years before, but it didn't take more than a comment about what had transpired for her father to explode.

'May I offer you some cake, Mrs Nairne?' asked her mother. 'Henrietta, you can pass the tray around.'

'Will Captain Cowin be joining us?' Mrs Nairne asked her husband as her thumb worked at a well-worn dent in the leather cover of her prayer book.

'Yes, I can't think where the fellow's got to,' Captain Nairne said, his laughter forced.

As Henrietta moved to the sideboard, she heard him mutter to Mr Babcock, 'Probably giving that young Betty a helping hand.'

The cake was already set out on the tray with the plates. Henrietta filled the glasses from the carafe of madeira. There was a faint shuffle of feet, then a coy giggle, and the door opened. As she took hold of the tray, she caught sight of Betty's heel disappearing down the hall. Her shoulders adjusted to take the weight of the loaded tray, and then she looked up.

Her eyes travelled up his broad uniformed chest, to the face of a god: her Apollo made flesh. The tray began to shake.

'Steady as you go, Miss Burbridge,' said the man. His low voice had a Scottish burr. 'You'll be losing your precious cargo.'

'Captain Cowin,' said Mrs Nairne. 'We were wondering where you had got to.'

Henrietta gripped the silver handles, now suddenly slippery. She bent to offer the tray to Mrs Nairne.

'That's lovely, dear.' Mrs Nairne took the tongs and proceeded slowly, far too slowly, to place several slices of cake on her plate.

Henrietta's arms ached. She glanced to where Captain Cowin sat. She froze, taking in the length of his legs stretched negligently before him.

'Is it from the latest shipment?' Mrs Nairne asked as she finally relieved the tray of a glass of wine.

'Yes, there was some fine madeira in the consignment,' said her father. It was the first time he'd spoken since Captain Nairne's mention of Uncle Herbert, her father's brother.

'Careful, Henrietta.' Her mother's hand moved under the tray to bring it level. 'Let's not lose the last survivors.' She began to tell Mrs Nairne the story of the disastrous breakage of their china and glassware on their voyage out from England.

Henrietta's knuckles were white and, with each step, the height of the gently sloshing wine rose against the sides of the glasses.

Her father waved her past.

Mr Babcock was still talking about whaling and sat with his stubby legs wide, his belly resting on his thighs. He outdid Mrs Nairne's appetite as he helped himself to cake.

One more step, then Captain Cowin.

'Just the madeira for me, lassie,' he said, before continuing to Captain Nairne, 'I never can understand why anyone would want to waste a perfectly good drop by mixing it with food, can you?'

Henrietta returned the tray to the sideboard and unloaded each item, straining to catch Captain Cowin's comments among the talk behind her.

All she could think about was how she could manage to see him again.

Chapter 4

Engage this roving treacherous heart

The previous night's rain had settled the red dust around St John's and everyone was smiling. Henrietta smiled with them, for there were red regimental coats everywhere, and she was sure that Captain Cowin was among them. Mr Babcock had attached himself to her side since the moment they arrived at the fair. Henrietta resorted to insisting that her sisters keep a hold of her hands to obtain some distance from him. Rose complained, of course, claiming she was old enough not to have her hand held. Nothing could spoil Henrietta's mood today, not even her sisters, hanging from both her arms, tugging her this way and that as they walked among the milling crowds.

'I wonder that the colony hasn't held an agricultural show before now, Miss Burbridge,' Mr Babcock said, surveying the scene with the air of an expert. 'Why, I've been to shows and then some, I don't mind telling you. There was one time I went along to the cattle show in Pittsfield, Massachusetts ...'

But Henrietta wasn't listening, as she mused instead on the possibilities of seeing Captain Cowin. She'd seen him on two occasions since the first time. Last time she'd even managed to say something to him.

It had taken her some time to decide what to say, and she'd been pleased with her question: *How do you find the weather here, compared with India?* But it had come out in a rush, and he'd not even noticed that she'd spoken to him until she'd said his name, and then she'd had to repeat it. She treasured his answer: *Here is not as hot as there, but still too hot by half,* turning the words over in her mind.

On the stock rails by their father's prize bullock, Bill and Griffith perched, glowing with reflected pride at the satin sash around its yoke. Leaving them, Henrietta glimpsed the top of her father's hat as he disappeared in the throng of men surrounding the governor. Through the crowd she glimpsed Uncle Herbert shaking the governor's hand. She hadn't seen her cousins anywhere.

Today of all days, she missed Eliza. With Eliza by her side, she'd be brave enough to go up to the soldiers and ask where Captain Cowin might be. The soldiers would think she was a child if her sisters were with her.

With Aunt Elizabeth now fully occupied with her new baby, and Mrs Burbridge's latest confinement entering its last stages, Mrs Nairne was charged with keeping an eye on them, as well as her own children, but her attention was wandering towards the needlework display.

Henrietta seized her opportunity. 'Mrs Nairne,' she said quietly, 'I worry that poor Mr Babcock may find the crafts not to his liking but is too polite to say so.'

'That's very considerate of you, dear,' said Mrs Nairne. 'Mr Babcock, please do feel free to join the other gentlemen. I'm sure the Good Lord did not intend that men should concern themselves about such matters. And we shall be perfectly safe amid the sewing and baking, I am sure.'

Mr Babcock spluttered and demurred for a little longer than politeness required and then, finally, made his excuses.

Mrs Nairne's face brightened at the sight of the sewing display. 'Now there you are girls, that's the sort of needlework you'll be doing in a few years if you are diligent,' she said. 'See the cunning little satchel that Mrs Morgan has made for her prayer book. Or this,' she said. 'Beautiful, just the thing for a young girl's bedroom. And what a suitable message,' she said, reading aloud, *'Beset with snares on every hand, in life's uncertain path I stand. Saviour divine, diffuse thy light to guide my doubtful footsteps right. Engage this roving treacherous heart, Great God, to choose the better part, to scorn the trifles of a day for joys that none can take away.'* As she read, she fingered the letters, attracting a glare from one of the women behind the trestle table. She then pulled her little boy's hand away, and said, 'Now, now, Jimmy, don't touch.'

'Over there, Henrietta, the flowers are over there,' whined Rose, wrenching her hand from Henrietta's.

Through the open flap of a large marquee, Henrietta caught a glimpse of towers of fruit and vegetables, and tables laden with vases of arranged flowers.

'Come on,' Rose said, 'Mrs Nairne won't mind — will you, Mrs Nairne?'

Mrs Nairne hesitated, gazing longingly towards the baking display ahead. 'Well, as long as you stay there, where I know where you all are.'

As they wended their way towards the marquee, Henrietta searched for Captain Cowin. This was the moment. It might be the only chance she had. There was a large group of soldiers gathered about the horse yards a short distance away, next to a roped-off area for the dressage events. The noise from the marquee rushed to meet her. Two steps inside and the heat rose, thickly perfumed by the sheaves of flowers and ripe fruit. She took one last look over at the soldiers. There, there he was, patting the large bay. Was he an entrant?

'Rose,' she said. 'You're in charge. Make sure that Beth doesn't wander off.'

'But where are you going?' Beth kept her grip on Henrietta's hand.

'I'll tell you later,' Henrietta whispered. 'We don't want Rose knowing, do we?' she added with a wink.

Beth grinned with delight at being included in the secret, and Henrietta slipped outside.

Getting over to the yards was harder than she expected. The crowds were rougher and louder and shoved more. There were fewer women, and the men watched her as she wriggled past.

'What's your hurry, girlie?' A beery face covered in whiskery stubble loomed into view before her.

Henrietta turned her head away and her ankle twisted on the rough ground.

An arm reached out, a strong hand at her elbow, and she looked up to see Captain Cowin.

'And what might you be doing out and about on your own, Miss Burbridge?' His voice was gentle but serious.

'I, I came to see the horses,' she stammered. 'Might I enquire whether you are riding today, Captain Cowin?'

'I'm a poor foot soldier, lassie, not a flash cavalry gentleman,' he said with a laugh, gesturing to the bay. 'She belongs to Allenby here, though not for long if his bets don't pay off.' He was directing the jibe more to Allenby than to her. 'Now you be running along back to your mother, little one.'

Little one, she bristled. She straightened up. 'It was a pleasure to have seen you again, Captain Cowin.' She held out her gloved hand.

The corner of his mouth twitched, but he bent low over it all the same. 'Maybe the regiment will return to New South Wales after our next tour in India, Miss Burbridge. If so, I look forward to meeting the young woman that you will become.'

India, what does he mean, India? Stunned, Henrietta struggled to think what to reply.

However, Captain Cowin seemed to consider their exchange to be at an end, for he resumed his conversation with the owner of the bay.

Her shock grew with each step back to the marquee. How could he be going to India? She lifted her hand, her lips touching where his lips had been only moments before. *Little one*, indeed. She reached the entry way and the smell of the ripening produce was edged with the sweet tinge of rot.

The combined weight of Rose and Beth nearly knocked her off her feet.

'Here she is, Mrs Nairne,' said Beth, her laugh laced with relief. 'Just lost among the boronias.'

But then, what were his words? *I look forward to meeting the young woman that you will become.* So, he wanted to see her again. All she had to do was to arrange it.

As the weeks went past, Henrietta's dreams and schemes for joining Captain Cowin occupied her every thought.

'Can we stop now?' Rose whinged. 'I'm sick of Greek legends. That's all we ever do. Why can't we draw the plants we collected yesterday?'

Their mother was preoccupied with their new baby brother, Edward, and predictably, the latest governess had decamped with their brothers' tutor, Mr Gilchrist. Henrietta missed his visits. He was a fine-looking man and was always so polite when she asked him a question of a scientific nature. Some nights, she had lain awake for hours trying to prepare some query for his next visit, just to have the excuse to stay longer with Bill and Griffith. However, whenever Mr Gilchrist came, she was shooed out to the drawing room to do needlework with her sisters and to practise her French. Of course, as good-looking as Mr Gilchrist was, he wasn't as handsome as her Captain Cowin.

'Look, Rose,' said Beth, 'I've been drawing Apollo in the land of the Hyper, Hyper—'

'Hyperborean,' Henrietta said with a sigh, now in charge of the lessons.

'Very-boring-ans, you mean,' muttered Rose, leaning forward to see Beth's drawing. 'Is that what those brown stick things are?'

Beth looked downcast.

Captain Cowin had already left with his regiment for India, and when Henrietta pictured him, which was at least several times a day, he was in a world very similar to the one Beth had drawn. Following her own train of thought, Henrietta said, 'No one knows where Hyperborea is. It could be India.'

'You just think it's India because that's where *he's* gone,' said Rose with a sneer.

Beth picked up her pencils again. 'When you go to India, Henrietta, you can write and tell us if there are any Hyperborean there,' she said.

'*You're* not going to India, Henrietta,' Rose said. 'Besides, Captain Cowin has already gone.'

'Mrs Nairne hasn't gone yet, though,' Henrietta snapped. Even as she spoke, she regretted it. Mrs Nairne's departure had been delayed, and Henrietta had taken it upon herself to become a regular visitor in her mother's absence. Mrs Nairne had grown to quite rely on her, or so she said to all their acquaintances.

The soft rub of Beth's pencil was the only sound in the room.

'You think Mrs Nairne will take you, don't you?' Rose said. 'Has she actually asked you?'

Henrietta shrugged.

'I can scarcely credit it, Mrs Burbridge,' drawled Mr Babcock. 'Whatever was she thinking?' He sat uncomfortably on the picnic blanket, his legs stuck out before him.

'A young girl's fantasy, Mr Babcock,' came her mother's reply. 'I daresay my own experiences in India coloured her imagination.'

This had quickly become her mother's standard comment when visitors chanced to hear of Henrietta's dream of accompanying Mrs Nairne to India. They usually learnt of it from her sisters' teasing. Rose in particular made sure to mention India at the slightest opportunity if Henrietta were present.

However, their mother's 'public' comments bore no resemblance to what she had said to Henrietta in private when Rose first told her of the scheme. Henrietta's ears burned with the memory. *'Foolish girl—what use do you think you'd be to Mrs Nairne—life of a camp follower—totally inappropriate for a young lady of your station in life—wait until your father hears of this nonsense.'*

Her father had been away looking at some land around Windsor with Bill. Endless days became endless weeks and, by the time he'd returned, Mrs Nairne had left for India. His face, always stern these days, grew darker on hearing the news of Henrietta's ill-judged obsession to go to India, but he had said nothing on the subject. This was worse, in a way. He spent all his time with her brother Bill by his side. Henrietta's place was with her mother and sisters.

In the weeks that had followed, Henrietta chafed at the restricted routine her mother had imposed: lessons, piano practice, a walk followed by an afternoon's needlework. She was barred from joining her mother on her social calls—'not until you can show me that you've developed some sense'—so Rose had taken her place. Griffith, deemed too young to join their father's expedition, had become her ally in devising ways to escape.

'Come on, Henrietta. Are you coming for a row or not?' Griffith's voice drifted up from the bank.

'Twist me round again,' ordered Beth, on the makeshift swing.

'Henrietta.' Her mother's tone was steady—neither a question nor a command—but her meaning was clear.

'Time to finish, Beth,' said Henrietta. 'If you spin any more, your pie won't stay down.' She gave Griffith a regretful wave.

'Do offer Mr Babcock some of your father's beer, Henrietta.' Her mother gave a nod in the direction of the space beside Mr Babcock.

Henrietta, kneeling, poured a mug. 'Mr Babcock?'

'Many thanks, Miss Burbridge.' Mr Babcock affected a notional bow despite the rigidity of his position created by the combined forces of his bulk and the cushions at his back. 'I must say, watching you at play with your sister is thirsty work.'

Henrietta forced a smile. Beth settled down beside her and took a large mouthful of pie.

'I hear you're quite the adventuress, Miss Burbridge. India, my word,' he chortled. 'But whatever would your mother have done without you? What would we, that is to say, Sydney society, have done without you? After all, there are so few young ladies of your pedigree, if I might be permitted the term in this context.' He paused to take a swig of his beer.

Henrietta leapt up and grasped Beth's hand, forcing the piece of pie out of her fist as she did so. 'Beth, are you unwell? You've turned green. Come away from the blanket.' She tugged Beth by her side. Beth's mouth was so filled with pastry as to make her protests inaudible.

Pedigree, as if she were one of her father's prize cows.

Behind her, she heard Mr Babcock recover from the interruption.

'Have I said something?' he asked, with a hint of impatience. It was the first time she'd heard him give any evidence of noticing her rudeness and, she had to admit, she'd given him plenty of opportunities.

'Not at all, Mr Babcock,' said her mother. 'Beth may have eaten a little too much pie.' Her voice hardened with every word. 'Henrietta will bring her back to join us shortly. I'm sure of it.'

Chapter 5

It's out of the question

Mr Babcock's presence precluded her mother from taking any further action that day. However, even the day after, her mother remained coldly silent. Henrietta watched her father closely at breakfast each morning, looking for some sign of the punishment to come for her rudeness to Mr Babcock. He glowered his way through the *Sydney Gazette*, grunted occasionally as he read the morning post, and only paused to reprimand Griffith if he fidgeted. Henrietta had almost begun to think that, by some miracle, nothing more would be said of her desire to go to India, when Griffith's fork dropped to the floor with a clatter.

'Griffith,' growled their father.

'For goodness sake, Griffith,' said her mother. 'If you fiddle with the cutlery instead of using it, then we'll have to take it away and you will have to eat with your fingers like some, some native.'

'Henrietta,' said her father, 'when you've finished your breakfast, come and see me in the study.' Still clutching the half-opened mail, he left the room.

Griffith, who moments before had looked cheerful at the prospect of being allowed to eat with his fingers, stared at Henrietta with his brow furrowed in sympathy.

Henrietta chanced a glance at her mother, but her mother's expression was guarded.

She cleared her throat. 'Might I be excused?'

The number of steps down the hall seemed to have multiplied. She stood in front of the door, steadied herself, and then knocked softly.

Her father sat at his desk. On the blotter between them lay a letter.

'Sit.' He waited, then said, 'I have here a letter from your Aunt Piggott.

Henrietta searched her memory. She had a number of aunts and they were forever writing letters. Her mother would read them out, giving all the latest news from Kent. Since Henrietta had last seen them when she was six, she could never keep straight in her mind which aunt was married to which uncle. She couldn't remember her mother reading out a letter from an Aunt Piggott.

Her father added, 'Your mother's sister.' He then corrected himself. 'Her half-sister, Elizabeth, married to a chap by the name of Arthur Piggott. Runs one of the agency houses associated with the East India Company,' her father continued absently, perusing the letter in his hands. 'Piggott, Davidson and Robertson.'

Henrietta already had another Aunt Elizabeth— Uncle Herbert's wife. It would be much too confusing to have to distinguish between two aunts called Elizabeth, she supposed, so this aunt had become Aunt Piggott.

'They live in India,' he added.

India. Henrietta's mind raced. Had her aunt met Mrs Nairne? Her heart lifted—Captain Cowin. But there her flight of fancy stopped.

'What I wish to know,' her father said, 'and I want the truth—have you been writing to your aunt?'

'No, no, I haven't.'

How could she, when she wasn't aware that she had an Aunt Piggott, let alone where she lived?

'For some reason, she has written to invite you to Calcutta.' Her father considered her for several long seconds. 'Go and see if your mother is free to join me.'

The full meaning of what her father had said didn't sink in until she had left the room.

The boat was small enough to be rowed by one person, but it was old and heavy and so it took the two of them to push it down into the river. Once the boat was afloat, Henrietta scrambled into the stern while Griffith dragged the oars out and manoeuvred them into place. He hadn't said a word to her since the letter had arrived from Aunt Piggott, so she'd been caught off guard when he'd whispered to her after breakfast to meet him down by the river.

No one would notice they were missing.

Griffith was left to his own devices most days when Bill was away with their father. Baby Edward was still recovering from whooping cough, so their mother was much pre-occupied. A new governess had still to be found, which meant that old Mrs James had been prevailed upon to come and sit with the girls while they laboured on their samplers. As usual, Mrs James' eyelids had grown too heavy to remain open, and her steady snores meant that they were at liberty to do as they pleased as long as they were quiet about it. Keeping Rose from telling tales would have been more of a hazard for Henrietta as she made her escape. However, Rose had developed a cough during the night and had not been allowed down to breakfast and was to stay in bed all day.

The chill of the morning was still in the air, and the light mist hadn't yet lifted from the river. Her cheeks felt soothed after the stuffy nursery and its over-stoked fire. 'For my rheumatism,' Mrs James had said of the need for warmth.

It was good to be away from the house, away from the tense admonitions of her parents. Her elation at her aunt's invitation had not been allowed to bloom. The conversation between her mother and father hadn't lasted long but, from what Henrietta could overhear from her vantage point in the hall, the offer would be refused. Henrietta had caught some of what her father had said.

'What do your family think they're up to? It's not as if your sister doesn't have children of her own. Do they think this will settle everything between us?'

All she could hear from her mother was an occasional low murmur. Afterwards, one glance at her mother's face had shown Henrietta that argument was futile.

Griffith still hadn't said more than the minimum needed to coordinate getting the boat afloat.

Henrietta decided to wait him out.

He rowed in silence upstream and around the river bend, then steered them out of the main current of the Parramatta River and into Duck River. It was little more than a stream, and the water was still and shaded. Out of view of the passing river traffic and obscured by the trees along the bank, it was their own private world.

He tossed the rope over a low branch and shipped the oars. 'So, India,' he spat out.

'And why would you care?' Henrietta stared at him. 'And besides, I'm not going. Mama said.' She adopted her mother's inflection. 'Your father says it's out of the question, young lady. He says you're far too young to be travelling alone to live with people you've never even met.'

'I don't believe you.'

'I'm not going, I tell you.'

'Then why are they still talking about it?'

Perhaps it was her question that made Griffith believe her.

He leaned forward, jiggling the boat with excitement. 'I heard them.'

'And?' Henrietta didn't want to hope. She'd hoped too many times over the last few months.

'Well, Mama said that you were running wild here—'

Henrietta gave a most unladylike snort.

'And that it was high time your education was taken in hand.'

'But I am educated,' said Henrietta.

Ignoring her, Griffith continued, 'And then more about being *finished* or something and how you were a gentleman's daughter, after all.'

'And what did Papa say?'

'Not much for a while. You know how he is.'

Henrietta nodded. Her father's silences were the longest and loudest of anyone she knew.

'But then Mama brought Uncle Herbert into it—'

'No,' gasped Henrietta.

'She said to Papa that the way Uncle Herbert was leaving cousin Eliza.' And here he did his own imitation of their mother. 'So bereft of accomplishments, it's a complete disgrace. And she

40

said something about no suitable marriage prospects here and how the only possible alternative is—'

'Is to send her, that is, me, elsewhere,' Henrietta said, taking in a deep breath. She clutched at the sides of the boat. 'Am I going? Tell me,' she screeched.

'Well, sounds like it, doesn't it?'

'You mean, you don't know? Then why were you all in a sulk?'

Griffith readjusted the rope as if to check it was still secure. 'Sorry,' he said in a small voice. 'It was only that …'

But Henrietta didn't have the heart to torment him—not when, impossibly, she might get to India after all. A vision of Captain Cowin's profile swam into mind. No, she wouldn't think about that now—not until she was sure.

'Of course you want to come too,' she said. 'There'll be Rajahs and palaces and …' She thought hard. 'Tigers. It'll be an adventure, a real adventure, and—'

'We'd be away.' Griffith's eyes shone.

Henrietta let her head fall back, feeling the sun's warmth on her closed lids. Winter sun was perfect. She wondered if Mrs Nairne was finding the sun in India to be *insufferable*.

She sat up and stared intensely at him. 'Education. That's it. Your education is as neglected as mine.'

'What?' It was Griffith's turn to snort now. 'Because I'm not being educated in dancing and sewing and some such useless stuff?'

'No, no, your profession. Whatever it is that you will be. Papa thinks it's going to be Bill running the properties, not you, or he'd be letting you go along with them, wouldn't he?'

Griffith mumbled, 'I'm too young to go along, that's all.'

'You're only a year younger, and Bill was allowed to go up to the Hunter with him last year.'

Clearly stung, Griffith tugged the rope from its mooring and thrust the oars into position.

Henrietta clenched her jaw. Now she'd thought of it, she couldn't let the idea go. If Griffith came too, then all the arguments about her travelling alone would be gone.

Henrietta bent low over the book in front of her. She was practising her French by reading aloud from *Les Mille et Une Nuits* to Rose and Beth, but she stumbled, her mind elsewhere. Rose and Beth were meant to be writing from her dictation, but her mistakes confused them.

'Sorry, sorry,' she said after Beth sighed despairingly from her smudged page.

'I'm not going to do any more,' declared Rose, putting down her pen. 'It's a silly story anyway. The genie won the heart of the princess, not Aladdin.'

'But Aladdin was the one who loved the princess,' said Beth.

'But the story says he was an idle good-for-nothing at the start,' retorted Rose, 'and he stayed that way; it was the genie who made things happen.'

Henrietta ignored their squabbling, glad of an excuse to stop reading. What she had to focus on was how to go about talking with her parents about India. Despite what Griffith had overheard, neither had spoken to her about it in the days since. Should she broach the subject with Papa first? He was the one who'd told her about the invitation. But she baulked at the idea. She'd have to talk to him alone, without any of her brothers and sisters around, or else he'd be sure to refuse to contemplate a change of mind, simply on the principle that a parent's word should never be questioned. The best place to find him alone was his study, but the memory of her last time in there was still fresh.

Perhaps I should try Mama instead? Unlike her father, the best way to get Mama to agree to something was if there were other people there, preferably visitors. But you still had to word it in the right way, so that it wasn't too apparent that you were scheming. So how could she raise it with her? She could ask her for one of her stories about India? No, too obvious.

'You don't get just three wishes, do you Henrietta? Henrietta?'

On hearing her name, Henrietta's attention turned back to her sisters.

'Rose says that the genie only gives you three wishes, but Aladdin made a lot more wishes than just three, didn't he?'

Henrietta, still not listening, gave a little shrug.

'It's a story, Beth,' Rose mocked. 'Wishes don't come true in real life.'

Beth was near tears.

Henrietta waded into the argument. 'Wishes can come true in real life.'

Rose stepped up to the challenge. 'You didn't get your wish, Henrietta. You didn't get to go to India to follow your prince.'

Mary appeared in the doorway, a cleaning rag still clutched in her hands and a smudge on her nose. 'If you please, Miss Burbridge, you're wanted in the drawing room.' She stuffed the rag she was holding into her apron pocket.

Surprised as much by Mary's unusual formality as by the request, Henrietta rose to follow.

Rose and Beth were silent but, the moment Henrietta was out the door, she could hear their whispered speculation start up behind her.

Mary followed her down the hall. Henrietta looked questioningly at her, but she gave a none-of-my-business shrug. Mary's nonchalance didn't hold as they approached the drawing room. She whipped out her cleaning rag and began to polish the oil lamp on the table that was right outside the door.

Henrietta couldn't restrain herself. She pulled up the cuff of her sleeve and gave the lamp a quick rub for luck before entering. She then stood before her parents, hands clasped behind her back.

'Your mother and I have been giving the matter of the invitation to join your aunt and uncle in India further consideration,' her father said in his slow ponderous way. 'As you know, we have been concerned for some time.' He paused before continuing, 'Some very considerable time, in fact, about the quality ...' He cleared his throat. 'Of education available to you here.'

Henrietta's fingers interlaced and unlaced.

'Of course,' he said, 'the lack of suitable educational institutions here is yet another matter about which the full disclosure of the relevant information was withheld, knowingly withheld, no doubt, by those who undertook to persuade, or rather, entice us to sell up everything we owned and migrate to New South Wales.'

The room began to spin and Henrietta remembered to take a breath.

'And in Calcutta ...' prompted her mother.

'And in Calcutta,' he continued, 'there's no doubt, no doubt at all, that there would be educational advantages for a young lady of your station.'

Henrietta fought back her smile. What if he wasn't going to say what she thought he was going to say?

'But.' He paused again, frowning. 'But, it's a costly business, this travelling to other continents. As far as I'm concerned.' He nodded in the direction of her mother. 'As far as we are both concerned, if the Piggotts want you to go to them, then they can send one of their own ships to come and fetch you.'

Her fingers locked together. How rich were the Piggotts? Was anyone so rich that they could send a ship to collect a niece they had never met? But wait— *one of their ships*? Were they that wealthy?

Her father seemed to have finished.

In the silence, Henrietta's mind raced. They were going to let her go. She would go to India. All it depended on was the Piggotts sending a ship. But then, with a stab, she thought of Griffith. Could she push her luck that far?

Her mother spoke. 'Your father is going to write to your aunt and uncle about sending a ship and,' as though reminding him, 'also about sending a respectable sort of woman to ensure your wellbeing for the journey.'

Her father nodded in acknowledgement.

'But,' her mother continued, 'I, that is, we wanted to ascertain whether this is something you really want.' She picked up momentum; the words rushed out. 'To be so very far from all the family you've ever known, it is a very difficult thing. You might never see your family again ...' she trailed off.

There it was, the opening.

'Perhaps,' Henrietta said, 'perhaps one of the others could come with me? I needn't be so alone then.'

Her mother hesitated, then, turning to her husband, said, 'We did wonder about sending Rose?'

'Rose's still very young,' interjected Henrietta. 'But Griffith—it might be good for Griffith's education too, wouldn't it?'

Her father leaned back in his chair and steepled his fingers. 'You seem to have given this some consideration, young lady,' he said.

Henrietta's hands were sticky while she waited for him to go on.

'Piggott, Davidson and Robertson are doing pretty well at the moment.' He seemed to be almost talking to himself. 'Not as well as some of the other East India Company's agency houses, but then ...'

Henrietta opened her mouth to add to her arguments, but her mother shot her a warning look and she thought better of it.

'If Griffith were to become … might be a good opportunity to have a trading partner …' Her father's voice died away.

Henrietta waited.

'I'll tell Piggott that he can take the two of you or neither,' he barked, on his feet in seconds, and strode out of the room.

The suddenness of his movement made Henrietta take an involuntary step backwards. Had she just ruined everything? She searched for some clue on her mother's face, but it might have been a mask for all the meaning that could be read there.

So much depended on the Piggotts.

Chapter 6

A pretty wee thing like you

As the *Eliza* was piloted out of the harbour, Henrietta and Griffith were determined to stay by the rail for as long as they could. Their boxes and trunks, still unpacked, waited for them in their cabins but there'd be ample time for that later. They could no longer see the rest of the family, as they were now just small dots of movement being rowed back to Campbell's wharf.

Beth had cried, but Rose had just kept dabbing with her handkerchief at eyes that looked remarkably dry to Henrietta. Griffith had shaken their father's hand with the solemn air of one sealing a contract, and then he'd whirled about to give her a grin that threatened to reach both ears. Her mother's lip had trembled, but all Henrietta could think about was the journey ahead. Soon, she promised herself, soon she would see Captain Cowin again. *I look forward to meeting the young woman that you will become.* She savoured the words. She might have turned fifteen by the time she next saw him. He'd take her seriously then.

She felt the August wind whipping her hair about her face and, next to her, Griffith had jammed his cap down around his ears to prevent it flying off to join the flapping flags at the stern. The sails wouldn't be raised until the *Eliza* reached the Heads, Griffith had told her. Captain Murray had already been obliged to admonish him for waylaying the seamen with his incessant questions. Griffith had been the same the whole way from England, Henrietta recalled, but he'd only been four then, so he didn't remember the answers he'd been given.

Back then, as they had entered Port Jackson, the dull-green scrubby promontories had dampened her excitement about their arrival. They had seen no houses, no people and, until the ship had followed the harbour around to the west, no other ships. Now, from the deck of the *Eliza*, she could match Griffith in naming each of the headlands as they passed. The olive-grey-mauve of the gums and the yellow dobs of wattle seemed in joyful harmony with the deep blue-green of the water.

'Watsons Bay, Henrietta, look,' shouted Griffith over the wind, which had picked up further. 'You watch, the pilot will leave us any minute now, as soon as we—'

There was an almighty crack as the sails swung around and ballooned into full stretch.

'We're off,' shrieked Griffith.

As the sandstone cliffs of the North and South Heads lined up on either side of the vessel, the pitching started.

'Time to be going to your cabins, dears.' Mrs Murray gently took Henrietta's arm, and Henrietta—

shivering now as the ocean spray rose—took Griffith's hand into her own and gave it a tight squeeze as they left the rail.

Life on board the *Eliza* soon fell into the rhythm she remembered from their voyage from England to New South Wales. However, on this voyage, she and Griffith were the only passengers and they ate each meal with Mrs Murray and her husband, Captain Murray, whenever he wasn't attending to his duties. They had sailed well out to sea, out of sight of land, in order to avoid the Great Barrier Reef, and the weather had stayed fine—so each day was much like the last.

Apart from meals, she saw little of Griffith. She had been under her mother's strict instructions to supervise him in the schoolwork she'd assigned them for the journey, but he was much more intent on learning every sailor's knot known to the first mate, Mr Bailey. He was also applying himself to learning the meanings of the different flag signals that the ship used to communicate to the other vessels they passed. Captain Murray took to calling him 'Captain Burbridge' and giving him a mock salute whenever he saw him. She watched enviously as he shimmied down the ropes to the jolly-boat and was rowed across with the captain to visit Captain Ashmore in the brig, *Hibernia*, which was heading in the same direction along with the *Derwent*.

Griffith's desertion meant that Henrietta spent most of her days in the company of Mrs Murray. She supposed that this was, after all, the reason Mrs Murray had come on the journey; however, it meant that apart from taking the morning air, they spent most of their day in the captain's cabin.

'Before we shift our course westward tomorrow, we'll have the pleasure of dining with both Captain Ashmore and Captain Carr,' Mrs Murray said. 'There won't be another chance for the rest of the journey.'

Henrietta looked up from her needlework, glad of an excuse to stop for a while.

Mrs Murray continued, 'I do wish they were travelling with their wives too, then there might not be so much drinking of spirits at dinner.' Mrs Murray was a strict Methodist, although Captain Murray seemed a rather more relaxed teetotaller. 'And,' she added, 'with some wives, we'd have some more female company for you.'

'The captains are both quite charming, Mrs Murray,' said Henrietta, who had been enjoying their attentions. 'I can assure you, I'm not conscious of missing a single thing.'

'Well, yes, I suppose they are rather gallant.' She paused with a smile. 'Particularly where a pretty wee thing like you are concerned.'

Henrietta tried to blush but, her cheeks remaining resolutely pale, she contented herself with dropping her gaze as she picked up her needle again.

In public, Mrs Murray was rather vaguely in her thirties, but she had confided in Henrietta that she had just turned forty. Mrs Murray told a very romantic story of the twenty years of engagement during which she had stayed on the Isle of Skye, steadfastly loyal to the captain, until their marriage earlier in the year. Henrietta rather thought this might cause people to do their sums and give the lie to her age.

'There the little fellow goes again,' Mrs Murray said, rubbing her belly. 'Whenever I'm sitting still, he starts his wriggling. Then the moment I'm moving about, he decides it's time for a nap.'

There had been some hushed conversations between her mother and Mrs Murray after she'd taken off her cloak and her condition became evident. All her mother had told Henrietta was that, as the journey progressed, Mrs Murray would need to rest more, so Henrietta should mind her manners and not be too demanding.

'You come from quite a large family, do you not, Henrietta?'

'Yes, I suppose so. There are seven of us, though that's not really very unusual, is it?'

'Your mother was telling me that she's been very fortunate indeed—never lost a single baby. She's a very lucky woman.' The lines on Mrs Murray's brow deepened.

Henrietta had never thought of this before although, now it had been brought to her attention, she supposed that it was indeed fortunate. She felt flattered that Mrs Murray was talking to her like this—it felt like the sort of conversation grown women had with each other.

'Um, I think my Aunt Elizabeth—Aunt Elizabeth Burbridge, I mean, not Aunt Piggott—may have, um, lost a child,' she said, 'or possibly, um, more than one.' She was thinking of Susan and Cook's chatter before little cousin Charles was born.

Mrs Murray gave her belly a soft pat. 'I'm sure this little one will make his way into the world just fine. And the ayah seems a most capable woman.' She glanced to the doorway where the Indian woman was sitting cross-legged in case Mrs Murray should need her. 'I mean, she came with the house.' She laughed awkwardly. 'The house in Calcutta that Captain Murray took for us for our married life together. And she said she was used to children. And she has been very diligent and attentive for the whole journey so far …'

'Will I have an ayah? I mean, just for me?' Henrietta thought of Susan and how the moment Henrietta could dress herself and do her hair in a plait, she'd moved her attentions to her younger sisters.

'Mm?' Mrs Murray mumbled, clearly preoccupied by her own thoughts. She then added, 'You would be quite comfortable, I mean, with all those younger children in the family, and … you would have been, what, already fourteen when Edward was born?'

'Thirteen,' Henrietta corrected her.

Mrs Murray nodded, but Henrietta wasn't sure she'd heard her. 'And the captain says that Mr Jenkins is a dab hand at physicking the men when they need it. Not that he's a real ...' Mrs Murray fell silent.

Uncertain how to reply, Henrietta was quite relieved to turn her attention back to her needlework.

'Are you sure there's nothing I can tell the ayah to bring you, Mrs Murray? 'Henrietta asked from the doorway.

Mrs Murray had remained in her bunk again this morning, complaining that sitting for any length of time was giving her a backache.

'No dear, thank you so much for asking. You'll have to amuse yourself, I'm afraid. I'm not very good company at the moment.' She heaved herself over to her side as Henrietta closed the cabin door.

Henrietta allowed the smile she had been repressing to spread over her face. Another day to herself, another chance to stay on deck. She brought her bonnet from behind her back, where she had been holding it while talking with Mrs Murray, tied the bow under her chin and clambered up and out onto the deck.

Seating herself next to Griffith, who was busily trying to splice two lengths of rope, she drank in the scene about her. There was enough of a breeze to keep the pace of the ship steady. Now they'd entered the

Torres Strait, the colour of the water had changed to an azure blue, intermingled with long stretches of aquamarine.

Griffith sighed loudly and pulled his ropes apart.

'No one helping you today?' she asked, amused at the expression on his face. It reminded her of the way their father looked when they weren't doing as they were told.

'Captain Murray says no one can be spared,' he said. 'With all these little islands and channels, they need lots of lookouts posted.' He pointed to the different sides of the boat, drawing Henrietta's attention to the sailors at different stations. 'And they'll have to be taking soundings, and we can only sail during the day, and—' He broke off sharply, standing up so abruptly that the ropes fell off his lap and onto the deck. 'Look,' he said, pointing to the fringe of palm trees on an island off to the starboard side.

Henrietta followed Griffith to the rail and then she saw them. Huge turtles lay sleeping in the sand. 'There must be …' She started to try to count them.

'A hundred.' Griffith was shouting in his excitement, 'A thousand.'

She chuckled. 'Well, at least one hundred.'

Mr Bailey joined them at the rail. 'That's where they go to lay their eggs.'

'Can we see one?' asked Griffith.

Mr Bailey grinned. 'You can *eat* one. It'll be turtle soup for the captain and his good lady tonight.'

They hung by the rails until the turtles were out of sight, and then they went to sit back down again. Henrietta was just thinking about what turtle soup might taste like when Griffith was on his feet again. At first she thought he'd spied more turtles, but there was a sudden rush of activity as the sailors hurried about. When she too followed the gaze of the sailors, she saw the hull of a vessel that was half-lying on its side, with just one end visible above the waterline, surrounded by jagged rocks.

'Shipwreck,' Griffith said, taking a deep breath. 'Can you see anyone in the water?'

Henrietta watched as they lowered the jolly-boat and rowed towards the wreck.

Unfortunately, on their return, the men were shaking their heads and looking grim.

Dinner was a quiet meal. Mr Bailey joined them, as the captain was still on deck and Mrs Murray had decided to eat in her cabin. Mr Bailey tried to lighten the atmosphere by teasing them about the soup, but neither Henrietta nor Griffith had much in the way of an appetite. For the first time, it struck Henrietta just how vulnerable they were at sea.

'They could have swum to an island, couldn't they?' asked Griffith. He seemed to be thinking along the same lines as Henrietta.

Mr Bailey looked doubtful. 'There are a lot of sailors who can't swim a stroke. They'd prefer the end to come quickly, rather than wait for the sharks.' Both Henrietta and Griffith must have looked shocked, because he then added hastily, 'But the ship's boat was missing from the *Morning Star*, so perhaps Captain Smart got them away safely. They left for Calcutta not long before we did, so it can't have been many days since … And the captain's posted watches for the rest of the afternoon and through the night. Maybe we'll spot a flag or a fire or something.'

Griffith could swim, even if Henrietta couldn't, she thought when she was back in her cabin later. Would he be able to hold her head above water for any time? She quickly dismissed the concern, as she was sure that Captain Murray would put her in the jolly-boat if they sank. She pictured Mrs Murray trying to clamber down the side of the ship. They'd have to swing her down in the hoist. But would there be time? She looked around the cabin, thinking about what she should try to save. She knew she should be sad; however, as she thought about the danger, there was a subtle thrill buzzing through her veins.

Sailing through the Strait was slow, and even the dazzling blue skies and glittering shallow seas full of darting fish had palled after a month. Her boredom was shattered when, late one afternoon, there was a loud banging on her cabin door.

'Henrietta, Henrietta, come quickly.' It was Griffith. 'They've found them! They've found them!' His footsteps faded off.

The air was damp in the fast-falling twilight.

'They've seen a white flag,' said Griffith, almost hiccoughing with excitement, 'on Booby Island.'

Henrietta caught a glimpse of tattered cloth, still being waved, high on a stick, surrounded by wheeling birds. The figure of the man waving it was barely visible in the darkening sky. From what she could make out, Booby Island was just a mound of rocks.

There were only five of them—sunburned, their eyes rimmed red. They stank of sweat, and Henrietta's eyes smarted from where she hovered with Griffith, doing her best not to be noticed.

'So, it could have been worse,' said the most senior officer. 'There's a kind of crevice in the rock with fig trees growing, so we had a bit of shade and a bit to eat.' He nodded towards a large, brawny man, who promptly spat on the floor. 'In the spittoon, Jones,' admonished the officer tiredly, before going on, 'Jones here, managed to catch a couple of fish.'

'Mr Hall, you say your captain and the other nine left in the longboat, what, five days past?' Captain Murray was writing an entry into his logbook.

'Yes, sir.'

'Aiming for Timor.'

'Yes, sir.'

'Well, the Lord willing,' said the captain, putting his pen down. 'Our second mate, Mr Davis, will be with you shortly to sort out your accommodation and duties while you're with us.' Closing his book he added, 'My wife is travelling with us to keep an eye on these young things.' He gave Henrietta and Griffith a quick smile. 'I need to see if she's any better. You two can make yourself useful and give these men more to drink while they wait.'

Griffith grabbed the large jug of grog and eagerly began filling the tankards the men held out, firing questions off to each of them, barely waiting for the answers. Henrietta followed with a jug of water, but had no takers.

'Now, girlie,' growled the man who Mr Hall had called Jones. 'I'd be betting there's a fine bottle of port in Captain Murray's cabin. How about gettin' us some?'

Henrietta coloured and looked to Mr Hall for guidance. He gave a sharp shake of his head. 'Did you build yourselves a hut on the island?' she asked, trying to recover from her embarrassment.

There was a low rumble of bitter laughter. 'What do you think we are?' Jones sneered. 'Somethink from *Robinson Crusoe*? Being wrecked i'n't some blooming tale from a book.'

Henrietta's hand holding the jug began to shake.

'Don't be embarrassing the girl, Jones,' interrupted Mr Hall.

'Not such a girl,' said Jones, leering. 'I've had y—'

'Enough,' barked the officer, getting to his feet as Mr Davis approached.

Chapter 7

Womanly mysteries

Over the weeks that followed, the shipwrecked sailor, Jones, seemed to always find work close by. Henrietta could feel his eyes on her from the moment she stepped on deck. She therefore became very attentive to Mrs Murray, confined to her cabin, just to escape the heat of his gaze. She couldn't wait until they'd reached their destination.

They were in the Bay of Bengal now, so any day now she'd be rid of him. He was the sort of sailor who could make a simple task stretch into a day's work, so he was always in trouble. After hearing Mr Davies send him below to work with the ship's engineer on the bilge pumps, Henrietta thought she might venture into the sunshine.

She peered out the narrow hatchway to check that the leering sailor was nowhere to be seen. She spotted Griffith in his favourite spot, unpicking a massive bundle of knots. The only sailors she could see were the ship's lascars bent over the brass fittings they were busily polishing. Her shoulders relaxed and she made her way over to him.

She'd brought her sketchbook and decided to attempt a portrait of her beloved Captain Cowin. The trouble was, however, the finer details of his face proved difficult to recall. She looked at her sketch critically—the nose was right, though the chin was weaker than she remembered, and what about those eyebrows? She screwed up the paper and cast about for inspiration. She started to draw Griffith as he sat talking about all things nautical.

'And then there's a system of flag signals that you can do with your arms.' His arms shot out like a deranged windmill. 'And—'

'That's not helping my sketch,' she protested. 'Have you thought about becoming a sailor, Griffith?'

He didn't answer.

She took the opportunity to have another attempt at Griffith's nose. It was a good strong Burbridge nose but, despite her best efforts, it was more tomato-like on the page.

'I don't think Papa would think much of that idea,' he said slowly, taking her comment seriously. 'Before we left, he kept talking about how a gentleman in a business like Uncle Piggott's could make his family's fortunes and—'

'If you were a rich merchant then you could own your own ship, or maybe a whole fleet of ships.' Henrietta put her pencil down to show Griffith his portrait.

He groaned. 'Your drawing isn't getting any better, Henrietta. It's worse, if anything.'

'Well, I could say the same about your knots, if I had a mind to.' She poked out her tongue. 'Perhaps I should try a landscape instead. I'll fetch my watercolours.'

'If you're quick, you might be able to paint those sea snake things.'

Huge snakes, as supple as leather, lay in the water below, knotted together in large wheels.

'We've been going past clumps of them like that all morning,' Griffith said casually.

They were the colour of tortoiseshell, shiny and glinting in the sun, varnished by the water that sloshed over their entwined bodies. They were beautiful but disgusting too, their shine slick and slimy.

A low cry from the direction of Captain Murray's cabin broke into her sleep. Then the groaning started again, louder this time. Henrietta had heard those sounds before. She'd thought her mother was dying and it had taken sharp words from Cook to stop her getting hysterical. 'Is just the birthing, you ninny, all perfeckly natchral,' Cook had said.

Mrs Murray lay awake as the hours passed, and the moans waxed and waned. Surely it would be over soon, Henrietta hoped. The ayah would look after everything, Mrs Murray had said so.

Suddenly, there was banging on her cabin door. 'Miss Burbridge, Captain Murray is asking for you.'

Henrietta couldn't see a thing in the darkness. She felt for her cloak, hanging by the door, threw it over her nightgown and opened the door a crack. It was Mr Bailey.

'Sorry to wake you, Miss Burbridge.'

'Is it Mrs Murray?'

'The captain asks if you'll come and give a hand.'

Henrietta didn't know what assistance she could possibly be for the ayah. Her heart was beating fast as she followed Mr Bailey's swinging lamp. What would she see? She was about to enter a womanly mystery and she wasn't at all sure she wanted to be initiated. She was only a girl. And what about the ship's doctor, Mr Jenkins? Mrs Murray had said he was a medical sort of man. Surely between Mr Jenkins and the ayah …

Mr Bailey stopped for a moment before the door. A piteous moan filled their ears. Mr Bailey's hand raised as if to knock, then it hovered till the moan died away. The instant his hand had struck the wood, the door was flung open. Mr Bailey moved aside for Henrietta to enter, and he backed away hurriedly.

The cabin was brightly lit by numerous candles and lamps, and Captain Murray rushed at Henrietta. Haggard and distraught, he spoke in a rush, his words barely decipherable.

'You must help, Miss Burbridge. I'm sorry, but you must help. The baby's coming too soon—we thought we'd make Calcutta before it came, but it seems that he's got other ideas.'

As he stepped aside, Henrietta's hand leapt to her mouth.

Mrs Murray lay curled on the bed in her nightdress, her face red and distorted with pain.

'But the ayah can help,' Henrietta whispered, looking frantically about the room for the woman.

'The wretch has gone to ground,' Captain Murray swore under his breath. 'We've combed the ship—she might as well as gone overboard for all I know.'

Mrs Murray gave a long low groan.

Henrietta could see Mrs Murray was doing all she could to suppress it. 'Mr Jenkins? Mrs Murray said he—?' she asked.

'In a drunken stupor with his new mate—one of the *Morning Star* lot, a blackguard by the name of Jones. They seem to have helped themselves to my port.' Captain Murray grasped her hands. 'Mrs Murray says you assisted at your brother Edward's birth. Please, you must help.'

Henrietta was so overwhelmed by his pleas that she found herself nodding mutely. She couldn't bring herself to tell him that the servants had bustled her off and the only help she had provided was to keep the younger children well out of the way.

'Thank you, thank you, there's water and ...' He glanced around the cabin, barely focusing. 'Cloths and the like.'

Mrs Murray groaned again, louder this time. Captain Murray gasped as if the pain were his own. He wrenched the door open and, his eyes filling, glanced back just the once before he left.

As Henrietta approached the bunk, Mrs Murray fell silent, panting. Her eyes remained shut, clearly savouring the pain-free moment.

Henrietta drew the chair closer and took her hand. A pang of guilt shot through her. Mrs Murray would be safe in her own home if it weren't for her mother's insistence on a female chaperone for the journey. Suddenly, Henrietta felt infinitesimally small, encased in a fragile tiny shell, bobbing on an expanse of ocean that stretched in every direction for miles upon miles upon miles.

She looked at the deeply etched lines across Mrs Murray's furrowed brow and thought of her mother's face. Her mother didn't discuss her own age, but she could only be a couple of years younger than Mrs Murray. Her mother had given birth to eight children and had been expecting another when they had left. Mrs Murray would be all right, Henrietta told herself.

'Mrs Murray? Is there anything I can get you?'

'Nothing, dear.' She closed her eyes again but kept talking. 'I'm sorry to have put you in this position. I'm afraid I rather exaggerated your experience to poor

Captain Murray—he was so wretched. Thank you for coming. We'll just have to muddle through together.'

Henrietta reached for a cloth and wiped the perspiration off Mrs Murray's face. She tried to keep her voice steady. 'Mama says that the baby knows what it's doing, so all you have to do is follow its lead.'

And, she thought, *Mama says that the first is the worst.* Henrietta had caught fragments of her mother's whispered tales swapped about the pain and agony. Her mother's story always ended with 'and she hasn't stopped causing me to suffer ever since' and a hard laugh.

Over the next two hours, Mrs Murray's cries grew louder and ever more frequent as she writhed on the bedding. Henrietta told herself it couldn't be too much longer. She felt completely useless. She bathed Mrs Murray's forehead and helped her into a fresh nightgown when the other had become sodden with sweat. She felt the bones in her hand grind against each other in Mrs Murray's grip. But as the long night wore on, Mrs Murray became weaker and even her cries dropped to a low, hoarse sigh.

As the grey of the dawn lightened the stern window, Henrietta tried to help her into a half-sitting position, holding a cup of water to her lips. 'Please drink, Mrs Murray. You must drink.'

But Mrs Murray's body became heavier, and Henrietta could no longer hold her as she sank back into the pillows. Henrietta turned to the table to put down the cup. Her head swam and she thought that she too might faint. Was there nothing she could do? Her gaze fell on the captain's bottle of brandy. 'Mrs Murray, here—try some of this. It'll strengthen you.' She cradled Mrs Murray's head and held the cup up for her.

The fumes must have jolted Mrs Murray into awareness. Her eyes flew open and she grasped the cup to guide it to her mouth. With astonishment, Henrietta watched as Mrs Murray, the strict teetotaller, drank the lot.

'I'll pour some more, shall I?' Henrietta turned away and refilled the cup.

From behind her, she heard Mrs Murray bellow with rage. 'It's time this baby was born.' Mrs Murray was sitting up, her arms stretched behind her in support.

Henrietta looked down at the cup, gave a quick shrug, and finished off the brandy before turning back to help.

The sun was well up when the bawling of the newborn brought Captain Murray back into the cabin. Behind him popped the head of the ayah, grinning broadly and bobbing her head up and down as she approached in a low crouch. Henrietta lay the baby in Mrs Murray's arms. Neither of them had had the strength to do much more than smile weakly at each other.

'No need to worry, Memsahib,' the ayah crooned as she took the baby. 'Very good with children, I am.'

Once Captain Murray had recovered from finding he was the father of a baby girl, he happily toasted her arrival with Henrietta, Mr Bailey, Mr Davies, Griffith, and with every sailor who wasn't on watch. And so it was Mr Bailey who received the pilot boat off Sand Heads and gave him the captain's excuses as the *Eliza* began the slow journey up the Hugli River towards Diamond Harbour.

Henrietta, sound asleep in her cabin, dreamed of sea snakes and eggs the size of turtles and, on waking, thought about marriage and wondered whether Mrs Murray might be wishing herself back on Skye. Strangely absent from her musings was any thought of Captain Cowin.

Mr Jenkins, once sober, pronounced that Mrs Murray didn't have a fever and prescribed bed rest. So Mrs Murray dozed in between feeds and, with the combined efforts of Henrietta and the ayah, the baby stayed clean and healthy. The Murrays had called the baby Henrietta. Henrietta liked to fancy that the name might have had some acknowledgement of her assistance but, as Griffith pointed out, Mr Murray's name was Henry, so perhaps not.

Little Henrietta only cried as much as any other baby Henrietta had known, and now—in the late afternoon—it was one of those times. The Hugli was broad and it had been two days before they could see the low banks on either side. The deck beneath her feet remained steady enough for her to risk taking Henrietta out on deck.

Griffith was aloft, moving like a monkey among the rigging. She doubted their mother would approve but then, she smiled inwardly, their mother wasn't here. The small bundled weight of the baby fitted the crook of her arm snugly and, as she sat and watched the large gold-red ball of the sun disappear, her mind was quiet.

Baby Henrietta gave a small wriggle and a tiny fist emerged with a jerk from her wrappings.

'Henrietta? Is that you?' Griffith's shadowy figure dropped down to the deck from the spar above. 'You were as still as a statue.'

Henrietta came to herself with a shake of her head. 'I lost track of the time. Mrs Murray will be wondering where I've got to.' She stood, and the ayah bustled over as if she had been waiting for her cue. So Henrietta relinquished the baby to her.

And oddly, Henrietta's arms felt light without her.

'I could see the lights from Diamond Harbour from up there,' Griffith said. 'We'll definitely be there by tomorrow.'

'Our last night on the *Eliza*.'

'I'm going to ask Captain Murray if I can toast the *Eliza* farewell.'

'With the captain's best brandy, no doubt,' she teased. 'You'll be acquiring a taste for it if you don't watch out, young Griffith.'

'Don't you *young Griffith* me,' he retorted. 'Besides, that's the pot calling the kettle black. I saw you the other night.'

They continued squabbling happily for the rest of the evening before heading to their cabins to finish their packing.

Chapter 8

You'll soon get used to it, my dear

Henrietta and Griffith stood on the wharf at Diamond Harbour, surrounded by their luggage. Everywhere they looked, brown-skinned men darted about carrying huge bundles on their heads. Some had fashioned a kind of cloth cup in the wrap of their turbans and swayed as they walked, not even needing to put a hand up to steady the load. Henrietta felt like she was in the middle of an ant nest with the lines of worker ants rapidly re-routing around them.

'There you two are,' bellowed a richly fruity voice.

Henrietta looked about, unable to find its owner. Then she saw him.

He looked like something from last century, with nankeen shorts that were cinched below the knee by large silver knee buckles, above white rubbed silk stockings. There were large buckles on his square-toed shoes as well, and he apparently suffered from bunions, because the straining fabric was slashed strategically for comfort. Wending his way through the milling workers, he came to a standstill before them, simultaneously mopping his brow with a large handkerchief and holding out his hand.

'My dears, so wonderful to have you with us. How was the journey? Are you both well?'

He didn't stop for a reply, and Henrietta gathered that this must be Uncle Piggott. Beside her, Griffith was shaking and, with a quick sidelong glance, she realised he was trying not to laugh. Looking at Griffith had been a mistake—it immediately became impossible not to giggle.

'Uncle Piggott,' she quavered.

'On to the *budgerow* with you, my dears. There it is, that one there with the row of blue cabins. Down the gangplank with you.' He began to dash about, directing the men about their luggage.

Confused, Henrietta looked around. There were hundreds of boats of every description moored at odd angles to each other.

'That one,' said Griffith, pointing, 'I think.' He was pointing to a long, flat barge topped by a structure that, under the dust and grime, might once have been painted blue. It lay alongside several other similar longboats moored side by side.

'Quickly, let's follow our bags,' she said, heading off after the men laden with their luggage.

This proved to have been a good idea since, after hopping across the gangplanks that formed makeshift bridges between the longboats, they found themselves on a different budgerow entirely to the one they had thought was their uncle's.

It took until late afternoon before the budgerow was poled out and away from its mooring. A simple square sail was raised to propel them against the current, and they continued their way further up the Hugli. By then, Henrietta's stomach was growling with the distant echo of a breakfast eaten at first light.

'What's this?' Griffith stared at the plates in front of them.

Uncle Piggott waved his hand about airily. 'You'll soon become familiar with it all, m'boy. My advice is to just tuck-in first and ask questions later.'

Griffith looked apprehensive, but he began to pile things on his plate. Henrietta was about to follow suit but, catching a twinkle in Uncle Piggott's eye, she hung back, wanting to see Griffith's reaction when he took a mouthful. Meanwhile, Uncle Piggott had started by tearing a large strip of round flatbread and taking a bite while spooning up something that looked like a lumpy pea soup.

Griffith closed his mouth on a large chunk of something that might have been mutton, which was coated in a reddish-brown gravy.

'Go easy on the Kosha Mangsho, m'boy,' said Uncle Piggott—the words muffled by the food in his mouth. 'It might be a trifle hot.'

Griffith's face began to change colour, from pale pink through orange to a deep magenta.

'Lot of spices, y'know,' Uncle Piggott continued conversationally to Henrietta. 'Not everyone's cup of chai. Your aunt's constitution is too delicate for it. Can take a bit of getting used to.' He took another bite of his bread.

Griffith's eyes were red and watering. He made the mistake of swallowing.

Henrietta thought he might explode. Beads of sweat had formed across his brow and were beginning to trickle down his face. She saw his mouth open and close, gasping like a fish. 'Water?' Henrietta thrust the mug towards him.

'Better to give him the raita.' Uncle Piggott nodded at the Indian servant who was standing behind him who promptly ladled a large spoonful of some thick, white substance onto Griffith's plate.

Griffith, mistrust imprinted all over his wet face, put a small spoonful to his lips. He closed his eyes then sighed with relief and took another spoonful, larger this time.

'That's the way, m'boy. We'll have you munching on whole chillies before long. Help yourself to the naan.' He gestured to the strip of flatbread in his hand.

Henrietta tried the raita first and also found that the lumpy soup, which Uncle Piggott called dahl, was delicious. Emboldened, she moved on to try the Kosha Mangsho and found, by dint of alternating mouthfuls with the raita and naan, that she quite liked it.

Griffith, still looking wary, followed her lead and was soon plying Uncle Piggott with questions about chillies and trying to establish just how hot they were.

With his stomach obviously full, it took Griffith no more than a second after lying down to drop off to sleep. Henrietta, too excited to sleep, her mind buzzing with her mother's tales of India, propped herself up by the cabin window and watched the tall stands of bamboo slide past.

The darkness was the blue-black of her bottle of Indian ink, and she found herself laughing softly having made this connection for the first time. Then she saw a small moving dot of light and then another, bobbing about, and then another. There were so many fireflies in and around the long reeds of bamboo that it was like watching fairies dancing in delight, their reflections on the still water making the edges of each ripple glow with a white-gold sheen.

By the time they finally reached Chandpal Ghat the next evening, Henrietta had become used to the sight of the local people in and around the riverbanks. Men, their chests bare and their legs swathed in a kind of long muslin wrap, stood knee-deep in the river checking nets suspended by long poles, or they were sometimes just standing and watching the boats as they passed.

But Chandpal Ghat was no rough set of steps—it was a structure of another order entirely. Lit by lamps, it rose steadily from below the surface of the river, its steps rising in large wide platforms to the level of the roadway, ornate archways forming the entrance way. In the darkness, Henrietta could just make out a large dome over the second storey. The whole edifice would have dwarfed any building in Sydney, and yet this was only the wharf. Henrietta tried her best to achieve insouciance.

'Quite something, heh?' said Uncle Piggott, standing with his legs wide for balance as the budgerow bumped against the steps. 'Some of these *babus* have more money than they know what to do with.'

Henrietta wanted to ask him what a '*babu*' was; however, before she had a chance, he was busy directing the men who'd clustered around the boat and were knee-deep in water.

The steps were teeming with people, some bearing burning torches and others holding lamps. Despite it being nearly midnight, there were boats everywhere and a rush of frenetic activity. Strong brown hands guided her along a rough-hewn gangplank then, once through the archways, she was delivered to Uncle Piggott who was standing chatting cheerily with Griffith. She took a deep breath.

'Now, never mind the smell,' Uncle Piggott said. 'It's a foreign country—you'll soon get used to it, my dear.'

Henrietta was getting the feeling this—you'll soon get used to it—might be a pet expression of her uncle.

'It's not nearly as bad as Sydney,' said Griffith, his eyes shining the reflected torch light.

It was a peculiar mixture of the familiar smells of fish and goats, as well as unfamiliar ones too, rich with cinnamon and spices she couldn't recognise, and all of those fragrances were overlain by the heady perfume coming from the enormous baskets of flowers piled behind her.

'Is it far to your house, Uncle Piggott?' asked Griffith, looking about for a carriage.

The streets were packed with people, and most of them seemed to have the leisure to stare. A cluster of street urchins had gathered about Henrietta, their little hands tugging at her skirts. She couldn't understand what they were saying, but their outstretched palms made their meaning clear. She began to fumble in her reticule for some small coins.

'Not far, m'boy, to Hastings Street, not far.' Uncle Piggott gave a click of his fingers and continued, 'But a little too far to be walking on my poor feet. Henrietta ...' He waved towards a sedan chair resting on the ground. 'Your aunt has kindly sent her palanquin for you. And Griffith and I will go by *doli*.'

From her seat in the palanquin, she could see Griffith following the example of their uncle in easing himself carefully into a reclining posture in a litter slung from bamboo poles that were borne by bearers.

The two men bearers carrying Griffith looked a lot happier with their lot than the four who bore the weight of Uncle Piggott.

Henrietta lost sight of him as, with a lurch, the palanquin bearers took their positions and hoisted her into the air. She clutched at the sides and ventured to look out the window. They passed rows of rough huts, leaned against each other for support, each with their own little cook-fire. The haze from the wood-smoke lay like a filmy gauze across her eyes.

As they moved away from the dock, even more people were in the streets—so many that she marvelled at the bearers' ability to navigate a route. The passers-by were so close against the palanquin's little window that she could have reached out and touched them. Every time they jolted to a stop, which was often, more children's hands filled the window in supplication. Their large brown eyes and snub noses reminded her of the Aboriginal natives, but she'd never seen their children on the streets in the night.

Stopping with a violent jerk, the palanquin bearers lowered her to ground. Had they arrived? She peered out through the window. They were still in the street. Ahead, a large light-brown cow was meandering past. It turned its soft eyes towards her in quiet curiosity. No one seemed to be herding it and it stayed there, meditatively. From behind her came a loud yell and, turning her head so fast she cricked her neck, she saw Griffith sprawled on the ground, the bearers bending to help him on his feet.

'Up you get, m'boy,' came Uncle Piggott's voice from somewhere behind Griffith. 'Only a little way still to go to Hastings Street. It takes practice, but you'll soon—'

Suddenly, large iron-wrought gates swung open into a cobbled courtyard off Hastings Street. In the glare of the torches, Henrietta found it hard to get a sense of the size of the house, but its brick walls glowed red, caught in the flickering torchlight.

'In you come, in you come,' cried Uncle Piggott. 'This way, this way. Your aunt sends her apologies that she can't come down to greet you, what with the new baby 'n' all. You can pay your respects to her tomorrow.' He sat down on a bench and stuck his feet out with a sigh of relief. Instantly, one of the servants bobbed down beside him, easing his shoes off and replacing them with richly embroidered slippers. He waved his hand in the general direction of a darkened recess. 'Your aunt has arranged for her own maidservant's daughter to be your ayah, Henrietta. Lakshmi will look after you.'

From the recess, a bowed figure shuffled forward, draped in white. Henrietta tried to make out her face, but it was obscured by the way she held up the end of the material that was loosely draped over her head.

Uncle Piggott stood and, clapping Griffith on the back, said, 'We can meet up with Henrietta back in the dining hall when we've all had a chance to freshen up.

We'll have a bite of supper before packing you off to bed.' He smacked his lips in anticipation.

As Henrietta followed Lakshmi, she estimated that it must be after one in the morning, but she was wide awake. After the fourth dimly lit corridor, Henrietta gave up tracking her bearings. Up endless flights of stairs and through doors, ghostly white figures swathed in muslin appeared and disappeared as they passed. The only sound was the tap of her shoes and the soft padding of Lakshmi's bare feet on polished wood. The back of her neck prickled and she pulled her shawl tighter.

Turning into yet another hallway, Lakshmi finally stopped and opened a door. 'Your room, miss.' As Lakshmi lit the lamp inside, Henrietta saw her high-arched eyebrows framing kohled eyes. She couldn't have been much older than herself. Her smile was shy. 'Here is what you will need, miss.' Lakshmi indicated the ornate pitcher and bowl behind a large bamboo screen, and then she disappeared.

When she was ready, she found Lakshmi sitting cross-legged on the rug outside ready to take her back to Uncle Piggott.

Henrietta's tiredness gave a brittle overlay to her nervous excitement. Shadows twitched in the corners of her eyes, and she feared losing sight of the ayah's shrouded figure leading her back through the maze of stairways.

Shafts of light from the dining hall streamed into the gloom of the corridor. Entering, she blinked in the blaze of lamps. Extending down the length of the room was a large teak table that would have seated more than twenty in comfort. The sides were flanked by double rows of marble columns rising out of the black and white marble floor. Fanning to and fro in a leisurely fashion above the length of the table was a contraption of canvas with pulleys, which were operated by a young boy near the wall. Intermittent eddies of air bathed her face as she walked slowly towards the figures grouped down at the far end.

At that distance, there were so many muslin-clad servants that it took her a moment to distinguish her uncle who, while still in European dress, was now clad in white. Beside him stood two other figures, similarly dressed. The shorter one looked to be similar in shape to her uncle. The taller of the two was regaling his listeners with some tale or other, as his features were animated and his gestures expressive.

'Henrietta,' Griffith called her over.

She kept her eyes on the Turkish carpet that led her to them.

'Wonderful,' exclaimed Uncle Piggott. 'Arthur, say hello to your cousin.' He waved vaguely between Henrietta and the short young man, who on closer inspection was revealed to be barely older than herself. 'Now we're all here, we can eat.'

At his clap, the places set for them at the end of the table were surrounded by plates heaped with food borne by silent servants, their turbans inclining as they retreated back among the colonnade.

Following his example, they slid into their seats.

Across from her, the storyteller cleared his throat. 'Now, young Griffith, I need to prevail upon you to introduce me to your sister. Mr Piggott seems engaged with other matters at the present.'

Uncle Piggott's cheeks were bulging with food and he gave a cheery wave to Griffith to go ahead.

Griffith's eyes widened at the responsibility then, his spoonful suspended mid-air, started off, 'Um, Henrietta, no, I mean, Mr Norton, um, Miss Burbridge, may I, um …'

The young man, taking pity on him, nodded politely. 'Alexander Norton at your service, Miss Burbridge. But everyone calls me Patrick.' He grinned at his own formality in such an intimate gathering.

It was impossible not to grin back.

'So, are you part of the family too, Mr Norton?' Henrietta asked.

His mouthful finished, Uncle Piggott chimed in, 'Patrick's on my side of the family, from the Glasgow horde. Can never remember which cousin's cousin he is though.' He waved his hand at her still empty plate. 'Eat up, eat up. You'll never be able to sleep with an empty stomach.'

As a servant began to fill her plate, Patrick's smile widened into a conspiratorial grin. 'And you're going to need all the sleep you can get to keep up with life in Calcutta.'

Chapter 9

Botany Bay flower

To Henrietta's disappointment, over the following weeks Calcutta did not live up to Patrick's prediction. Aunt Piggott was a fretful woman who spent her days fussing over her newborn or stretched out on the chaise-lounge complaining. And as Aunt Piggott's indolence made her highly sensitive to lack of industry in others, Henrietta and Griffith had been added to the list of her complaints.

Luckily, they quickly found that the large verandah overlooking the garden was one of the few places they could escape her watchful presence. Her time with Griffith was precious, as he generally had lessons with his tutor in the mornings. In contrast, Henrietta's continuing education turned out to consist of dance lessons, with a view to attracting the eye of a suitable suitor.

Cousin Arthur was assigned to accompany her to the dance lessons. 'Can't stand dancing,' he confided, 'but Mother thinks my social manners need brushing up before I head back home to school.'

The class was held in the old government house, locally known as The Palace. It was so close to Hastings

Street that they could have walked the distance in ten minutes, but Aunt Piggott insisted they take palanquins. The others attending the class were mainly young ladies who were either out or nearly so. There were some boys other than her cousin, which Henrietta had been surprised to see. However, she couldn't bring herself to think of them as 'young men' since, although of an age, most were barely shaving. A few looked pleasant enough, she supposed, but the other young ladies in the small class had already formed their alliances and so she found herself assigned to her cousin. As well as having a tendency to perspire, Cousin Arthur was a head shorter than her.

At the signal from the dance mistress, the elderly Miss Desacourt struck the first notes of the accompaniment. The piece she was playing was rendered unidentifiable by her slavish adherence to the metronome. Henrietta tried to block the sight of the beads of sweat gathering on her cousin's upper lip and, instead, imagined she was her grandmother, young Elizabeth Carter, gaily captivating the dashing Louis de Perroquet.

'You are looking *très charmant*, this evening, *mam'selle*,' whispered the Count in his French accent. '*Entre nous*, I came especially tonight in the 'ope I would see you.'

And her grandmother would say—Henrietta tried to think a reply worthy of someone with *jeu d'ésprit*.

Cousin Arthur interrupted her thoughts, and said, 'So what is Botany Bay like?'

She acknowledged the comment with a small smile. Aunt Piggott had already asked her the same question. Her enquiry had carried with it a hint of a scornful sniff with a tinge of vicarious excitement.

The cotillion progressed and her cousin seized his next conversational opportunity. 'You must love being out of the prison, as it were?'

'Calcutta is perfectly delightful,' Henrietta replied, essaying the sort of icy tone she so admired in her mother's dealings with disagreeable comments.

Cousin Arthur, however, was impervious. He stayed by her side despite her best efforts to shift him. A young blonde girl, who had been holding court to her coterie in the corner, disengaged herself and approached.

'Your cousin is most attentive,' she said, 'but don't worry, all the boys get shipped back home to school next month.' She gestured vaguely in the direction of the boys grouped together at the other side of the room.

Caroline was older than she had first appeared. As a skilled gossip, she was the one who was always in the centre of the conversation.

She hooked her arm through Henrietta's. 'Go and talk with the other young gentlemen, Master Piggott, there's a good boy. We need to discuss what we are wearing to the governor-general's ball.'

Relief flooded Henrietta. Back in Sydney, she'd known all the families they mixed with in the colony, and she was the one who usually served as the social pivot for her friends and cousins. To stand on the outside had felt more like prison than any penal settlement.

But dancing lessons couldn't fill the whole day. She wasn't used to staying indoors for such extended periods. The afternoons dragged, as she rarely saw Griffith then either. After his lessons were over, he got to accompany Uncle Piggott when he went about his agency business.

One afternoon, Patrick had dropped back home from the Writers' Building to deliver some documents for Uncle Piggott to sign when he returned from his visits. Catching sight of Henrietta's forlorn expression, he said, 'Cheer up, Miss Burbridge.' He blew on his tea to cool it. 'Whichever boy you're pining after is sure to notice you soon.'

She rolled her eyes. 'It's nothing to do with a boy.'

That was the trouble with Patrick. It was more fun when he was around, but he seemed to think it was funny to ignore that she was fifteen now.

'I don't care how hot it is outside,' she exploded. 'I want to get out. I don't see why I can't go for a walk. I could go shopping. My Hindustani is good enough for that. Or I could go with Lakshmi. It would be perfectly respectable. Lots of Indian ladies walk about together.'

Patrick cast his eyes to the ceiling, in the direction of Aunt Piggott's rooms. He didn't need to say any more.

Henrietta had been subjected to a close inspection by her aunt the day after her arrival, and she'd made her views known. 'I don't know what your mother let you do, but while you're in my care ...' and 'your skin is already positively ruined, ruined my dear, I don't know what your mother has been thinking' and 'it's not safe, you know, India is full of cut-purses and rascals' and 'if we were back home in England, things would be different. In England ...'.

In England, as far as Aunt Piggott was concerned, everything was perfect—the weather was perfect; the food was perfect; the people all spoke English, and of course that meant they were all perfect too. England was 'home'.

'Tell you what,' said Patrick, 'how about I ask Mr Piggott if he'll take you along with Griffith sometime?'

Griffith had painted a less than enthusiastic picture of life tagging along with Uncle Piggott: 'all bowing and drinking tea and sitting still and talking endlessly about how Piggott, Davidson and Robertson can build its trade with Canton'.

She nodded doubtfully.

'And you'll be driving The Course this afternoon, won't you?' Patrick asked.

'Stuck in the carriage, though. You could ask her if I could ride, couldn't you?'

Patrick rose to leave. 'There's a ball coming up. Why don't you ask your aunt if you can go? Tell her I'll keep an eye on you, if you like.'

She'd expected her aunt might arrange her introductions, but Aunt Piggott proved to be a most unsociable woman. Uncle Piggott insisted that his wife take the carriage out each afternoon for fresh air; however, that was the limit of her outside activities.

Driving 'The Course', as everyone called it, was a daily ritual in Calcutta. It was out of the question to go outside during the middle of the day so, in the late afternoon, the women would take their places in the grandest of their family's conveyances, and their husbands would mount their best horses and trot alongside in a chaotic procession of finery as the locals flitted in and out of the traffic like birds of paradise. Once Griffith had demonstrated his horsemanship to Uncle Piggott's satisfaction, he was allowed to ride. Henrietta sat squashed beside Aunt Piggott who, perked up by the bustle, condescended to attend to her.

'Where's Arthur got to?' her aunt asked imperiously.

Henrietta watched with dismay as her cousin bounced towards them on a fat, dappled mare.

'Glad to see him getting some exercise.' Aunt Piggott said. 'I told him to accompany you to your dance lessons. I hope he has been doing so?'

'Yes, Aunt. I'm glad of his company.'

'I hope he talks to the other young ladies. You aren't monopolising him, I hope?'

'No, no. We talk with Miss Caroline Walker,' Henrietta said defensively.

'Ah yes. No cash flow, but the family assets suggest potential inheritance.'

'Um, Miss Walker was asking if we're going to the governor-general's ball.'

'Oh, that. I wasn't thinking of going; it's all a bit of a bother really,' Aunt Piggott said. 'And you'd need a chaperone. I'm not at all sure your uncle will be back from Agra in time.'

Henrietta stared ahead at Cousin Arthur's rump bumping along in the distance. 'Cousin Arthur could go. And Patrick, I mean, Mr Norton, said he'd be happy to come along.'

'I see you've given the matter some thought,' Aunt Piggott said acidly. 'I'm not sure Mr Norton's cut out for such a role, mind. An eye for the ladies, if you ask me. You'd be lucky to see him again after the first dance.'

Henrietta sought to keep her face calm. She didn't want her aunt to think it mattered.

Their carriage had made the last turn before her aunt spoke again. 'Perhaps, it's not a bad idea for you to attend. Reverend Bryce told me he was planning to go. I'm sure he'll be happy to keep an eye on you. Do give the Walkers my best regards when you see them.'

The finality with which she said this brought the subject to a close. Henrietta thought of her mother and the hours they would have spent discussing her choice of dress, perhaps even having one made specially.

'Henrietta, dearest, take the red shawl,' she'd say, 'the one that Baroness Imhoff gave me when I left India as a child. It will go so well with your complexion.'

The sky purpled into twilight. The globe of flame swayed as the torchbearer ran ahead to light the carriage's way, and the *bheasties* scattered water to settle the dust. She blinked away the first moist damp of dew.

The guests were arriving and the hum of voices filled the entrance. In the heat, the smell of the women's perfume settled like steam over the heads of the crowd.

Reverend Bryce took Henrietta's arm to steer her along the reception line as it inched its way to the governor-general, Lord Moira and his wife, the Countess of Loudoun. Over the shoulders of the people ahead, she glimpsed the hosts for a moment then the line edged forward and she lost sight of them. Her knees sagged.

Perhaps Reverend Bryce felt her tremble, since he said in a low voice, 'You don't need to worry about a thing. He's a man like any other.'

From behind, Patrick whispered, 'You'll find it easier if you keep breathing.'

She held her last remnant of air as she heard her name and then she was there.

Introductions were made, but she heard none of them. Instead, she found her attention caught by Lord Moira's expressive face as he talked with Reverend Bryce.

'I hear from Bishop Middleton that there was much ecumenical debate on your journey out, Reverend Bryce. I didn't think to see the day when a Presbyterian would see eye to eye with an Anglican,' he said with a smile.

'Not so much agreement, I must say. Perhaps spirited competition might describe it better,' replied Reverend Bryce.

Then Lord Moira's gaze turned to her.

'Ah, I see the reports were accurate, Miss Burbridge,' said Lord Moira, chuckling. 'You are quite the Botany Bay flower. I've no doubt it won't be long before some fine gentleman seeks to pluck you to press between the pages of his collection.'

His wife tittered with embarrassment. 'Don't listen to a word he says, Miss Burbridge. He can be such a rogue in the company of young women.'

The press of the guests moved them into the main ballroom. The room was immense—Henrietta couldn't make out the faces of the people at the far end. The chandeliers were thick with candles, their blaze so bright she couldn't look at them. The silks and satins of the women's gowns shimmered in the light against the dark colours of the officers' dress uniforms and the coats of the gentlemen—some fashionably black, others richly-embroidered in the old style.

'What did you mean by "spirited competition", Reverend Bryce?' she asked.

'Ha, you caught that, did you? Well, your Bishop and I are both in the business of building churches for our congregations here in Calcutta, Miss Burbridge. However, the good Bishop was at considerable pains to point out that plain Presbyterians such as myself build mean churches without so much as a spire to draw the eye. So I vowed that the Scottish Kirk in Calcutta will have a spire, higher even than that of St John's, even if I have to put a weathercock atop it.' He kept talking as he steered her through the crowd.

Henrietta lost track of Patrick while the Reverend introduced her to all and sundry as they passed: Mr So-and-So and Mrs So-and-So, and the Misses What's-her-name. She barely heard the names, and she forgot those she did catch within seconds of meeting the next ones. He was clearly determined to discharge his duty as chaperone to his full capacity and, since he knew most of the British community, this meant she was in danger of being introduced to more than half the room.

He checked their progress after a while to introduce her to Sir James Caldwell and his wife, who were standing with Mrs Winterbottom and her five buck-toothed daughters. They were grouped about old Miss Prendergast.

'First time in India, I take it?' asked Lady Caldwell, her voice like cut glass.

'Of course it is,' said Miss Prendergast. Henrietta had to lean in to hear her words. 'That is, unless she came here when she was as young as her grandmother.'

Excited, Henrietta blurted, 'Did you know my grandmother, Miss Prendergast? What was she like? I never met her; she died when I was still very young.'

'She was a talker too.' Miss Prendergast wheezed. 'Like grandmother, like granddaughter, it seems.'

'Miss Prendergast is a walking history book,' cut in Reverend Bryce. 'Ask her about anyone from the early days in Calcutta and she knows them, or if she doesn't, then she knows who they married.'

Miss Prendergast preened, her bent back straightening as far as it could.

'Knew Governor Hastings, didn't you, Miss Prendergast?' said Lady Caldwell in the loud tones that people adopt when addressing the elderly. 'And that appalling woman he finally got around to marrying.'

'Baroness Imhoff?' Henrietta asked. She knew she shouldn't speak again so soon, but Lady Caldwell's description jarred with the glamorous image Henrietta had formed from her mother's stories.

Miss Prendergast began to laugh, but it caught in her chest and she gave a violent cough instead. 'Heard the story of the romantic voyage, then have you, girlie? How she nursed him back to health through the stormy seas?' Her voice was so faint that Henrietta was reading her pruned lips.

'I'm sure we don't want the young girls hearing such tales, now do we?' Mrs Winterbottom glanced to her daughters, whose eyes were wide.

'Ah, there he is,' Reverend Bryce exclaimed, staring off to the other side of the room. 'If you'll excuse us, ladies, Mrs Piggott especially instructed me to introduce Miss Burbridge to Mr Martin.' He extricated Henrietta from the gossipers and led her through the crowd, nodding genially at a number of his acquaintances as they went past.

Henrietta tried to see past his broad back to glimpse where they were headed. His destination appeared to be the French windows along the side of the room. Perhaps it was the convenient proximity to the open air that made the gentlemen cluster there, as she could see through the doors men smoking while they strolled about in twos and threes on the balcony.

Close by was a group of young officers standing about, casually conversing. Their bearing reminded her of Captain Cowin, not that she cared. She was older now, fifteen, not a silly girl chasing after anything in uniform. With Revered Bryce forging his way through the crowd, she had to tap him on his shoulder to get his attention.

'I think I see some friends of an acquaintance of mine,' she said. 'Do you think we might head over so that I may make enquiries?'

Reverend Bryce looked to where she was indicating and his eyes crinkled. 'Ah, they look very fine in their uniforms, to be sure. But I can't be confessing to your aunt and uncle that I let you talk to an officer without an introduction, now can I?'

'But, you could—'

Reverend Bryce quickly took her arm and steered her away with gentle determination.

The officers' eyes were bright with alert watchfulness. They paid scant attention to what their fellows were saying, their gaze flitting across the pretty young women, alighting here or there.

Near the officers, she could see Patrick talking with a group of gentlemen about his age. Like them, his posture was more erect than usual, as if mirroring them. Manliness was more than a red coat, the stance of the gentlemen said. They were more discreet than the officers. They looked about the room only intermittently, their gaze directed as if searching for someone of their acquaintance, but their eyes lingered on the young ladies. She was conscious of being among the momentary pinpoints of their searches. For the first time, she caught a glimmer of what it must have been like to be her grandmother—to shine.

Reverend Bryce came to such an abrupt stop that Henrietta almost ran into him. He'd stopped before a group of older gentlemen standing together, their legs planted wide and their hands resting on their waist-coasted bellies: widowers, perhaps, or men who'd sent their wives and families home to England; or never-married confirmed bachelors, content with their port and cigars. *Not one of them*, she hoped. Surely her aunt wouldn't consider any of the old men as prospective suitors?

'Now, Miss Burbridge, I have great pleasure in presenting an old friend of your aunt and uncle, Mr Martin.'

'Delighted, Miss Burbridge. So pleased to make your acquaintance,' said a man dressed in a white jacket and waistcoat. He swirled his hand in an old-fashioned flourish as he bowed low—so low that his baldpate was revealed, shiny in the light cast by the chandelier above. Circling the polished surface was a fringe of long, grey hair tied back in a cue with a black ribbon. 'But really, Dr Bryce, I must object to the epithet: *old*. I do own to knowing the Piggotts for some years, but surely, we are all only as old as we feel.'

Mr Martin reminded her of Uncle Piggott, with his nankeen breeches clipped tight with buckles that matched those of his shoes. He did have better legs than her uncle, which was fortunate since his garish pink ribbed stockings drew the attention in that direction. Civilities exchanged, he bowed again. Henrietta heard the faintest creak of his knees as he straightened.

'I hope I may have the honour of a dance later in the evening. I'm still sprightly enough to step a tread or too, despite the good Reverend's aspersions.' He waggled one pink-stockinged leg in demonstration.

She was spared an answer as Mr Martin was distracted by Caroline and her mother joining them. Mrs Walker displayed the family's wealth in the heavy strings of gemstones that wreathed her considerable expanse of bosom.

In the middle of introductions, the orchestra struck up for the first set of quadrilles, and the floor cleared as the principal ladies of Calcutta society took their places with their partners.

As they watched, Caroline whispered, 'They make our efforts at dancing lessons pitiful, don't they?'

Henrietta couldn't help but agree. Their grace and precision were superb. She resolved to practise more often. One day, she would be among the finest ladies in society and everyone would admire her as she danced with her handsome and important husband.

'Your Mr Norton is rather good-looking, don't you think?' Caroline murmured, glancing in Patrick's direction.

Henrietta caught the question that lay beneath. 'He's not *my* Mr Norton,' she replied. 'I can't say as how I've noticed what he looks like.'

Caroline smiled with satisfaction and dropped her eyes coquettishly in Patrick's direction.

As the music shifted to its close, Henrietta realised with panic that Mr Martin was moving away from the other gentleman and looking in her direction. She glanced about for Patrick to help her escape, but he'd taken the floor with Caroline.

Cousin Arthur stood by, awkwardly rocking forward and back on his toes. 'Miss Henrietta,' he said with a puff. 'Um, do you think …?'

'Of course.'

When she'd imagined her first dance at a ball in Calcutta, she'd pictured dancing with an altogether different partner. But, she consoled herself, she was in Calcutta, and she was at a ball, and she was dancing. By the end of the set, Henrietta had revised her thinking. She was exhausted with steadying herself alongside her cousin's lurching motion through their turns. She was only too ready to accept his suggestion that they seek refreshment.

Entering the supper room, she was content to take in the scene as he went to fetch her some punch. She caught a fragment of the conversation behind her.

'I'm sure I don't know what Miss Walking can be thinking,' said Lady Caldwell.

'She is certainly a catch.' It was old Mrs Prendergast speaking, and Henrietta had to strain to hear.

'Mr Norton is completely aware of that fact, I'm sure,' replied Lady Caldwell.

Miss Prendergast replied, but she was too quiet for Henrietta to hear.

'No, he has no prospects whatsoever,' Lady Caldwell answered. 'Totally reliant on Mr Piggott's goodwill. Lucky to have obtained his position as a clerk, if you ask me. Miss Walker thinks to play with him, no doubt. But she's a foolish girl if she doesn't realise the effect such idle flirting has on her prospects. Any right-thinking gentleman in the room will pass her by after such a display. Two dances, one after the other. Well, I ask you.' Lady Caldwell sniffed.

'And Miss Burbridge is staying with the Piggotts?' she heard Miss Prendergast ask.

'Very kind of Mrs Piggott, in my opinion,' harrumphed Lady Caldwell. 'Very kind indeed. It's a hard job trying to find a husband for a girl, particularly one who ...'

Maddeningly, Henrietta missed the rest. *A girl who, what? Talked too much?* She thought of her grandmother's skill with *repartée* and sighed.

'I'd say that Mrs Piggott might have her eye on Mr Martin for Miss Burbridge. A much better prospect,' Lady Caldwell responded to the inaudible Miss Prendergast. '£1,000,000 sterling, Sir James tells me.'

Her voice rose again to its normal clarity in reply to a comment from the old lady. 'Tosh. He's only sixty. She won't do better than him in Calcutta, I mean, considering ...' She left it there, her voice tinged with implication.

A burst of titters from the Winterbottoms drowned out their next few comments. Henrietta glared at them.

'No, no. My dear Miss Prendergast, I'm sure it won't wash off. She's spent too much time in the sun, that's why she's that bright colour. No doubt, she's been let run wild in New South Wales. There's no real society there at all, you know. I hear that their servants are convicted felons. Well, I ask you, what kind of place is that to bring up a young girl? No wonder ...'

But Henrietta didn't find out what Lady Caldwell wondered, as Cousin Arthur arrived with her drink — or what was left of it, after he'd jostled his way through the throng to give it to her.

She held the cool glass to her cheek. If her complexion had been thought unseemly before, now it was blazing with vulgarity. She wanted to be anywhere but here, anywhere but at the ball, anywhere but Calcutta.

'Miss Burbridge? Are you feeling all right?' Cousin Arthur asked.

'I'm fine,' she said and, as she uttered the words, she realised she was indeed perfectly fine. She set her jaw. *How dare they? Two old biddies, with all the sap of life drained out of them.*

'Are you up to another dance?'

His hope was painful to hear.

'No, I think I may have danced enough for one night,' she replied, 'but let's go and see if we can find Miss Walker.'

They found Caroline at the centre of a cluster of her friends, all giggly with too much punch and darting dangerous glances at their admirers. Cousin Arthur was inveigled by Mrs Winterbottom to dance with each of her daughters in turn, to the mutual unhappiness of all concerned.

Patrick was nowhere to be seen. What had happened to his promise, 'I'll keep an eye on you, if you like?' Her toe tapped with irritation at first, and then, caught by the insistence of the melody, along with the music.

'You're not dancing, Miss Burbridge?' Mr Martin asked, appearing beside her.

'No, thank you. But I've danced quite enough, I think, for one evening.'

'Very wise of you. Overexertion in this climate can prove injurious to the health. The blood rushes to the head and can inflame a choleric nature.'

This was too close to the thrust of Lady Caldwell's comments about Henrietta's complexion for comfort. She concentrated on watching the dancers. Mr Martin remained by her side, effectively discouraging any other potential dance partner from approaching.

Finally, Reverend Bryce tore himself away from the supper table. 'Well, I've finished my rounds of the parishioners,' he joked, 'and I see Mr Martin has been taking good care of you. But with dawn not far off, it's more than time we got our lovely Botany Bay flower off to her slumbers.'

It was only the Reverend, Cousin Arthur and herself in the carriage on the way home. Patrick must have found entertainment elsewhere, but she was too tired to care. She thought of the words that the governor-general had said to her in the reception line.

An image flooded her mind of her sisters pouring over their flower collection: picking the finest blooms — no bruised petals, no pollen yet blown away by the wind — pressing them carefully between thick sheets of absorbent paper before closing the book slowly, so as not to shear the flattened flower; checking the pressing process as the days went past; evaluating the faithfulness of the two-dimensional version of the living beauty that once had been; until finally, entering the desiccated remains into their catalogue of botanical acquisitions.

Chapter 10

The loveliest houri

Patrick might not have turned out to be much of a chaperone, but he did manage to convince Uncle Piggott to let her come along when he made one of his business calls with Griffith. Their carriage followed the gravel drive that swept in an arc through lush lawns to the *babu*'s house.

As Henrietta stepped out of the carriage, silence enveloped her. The house was surrounded by dense foliage, screening it from the noise of the busy street. It had three storeys and was fronted by large marble columns along its length. She hung back behind Griffith as they followed Uncle Piggott inside. Entering the vestibule, her eyes took a while to become accustomed to the dim light. The tiles on the floor were marble—cool white, rose, and grey. As they moved towards the inner courtyard, a gentle waft of air greeted them, bringing with it the calls and songs of birds.

'There's an aviary,' Griffith told Henrietta. 'I can show Henrietta the birds, can't I, Uncle Piggott?'

This was unusually polite for her brother. Henrietta assumed he'd used the birds on previous visits as an excuse to avoid the tedium of the men's talk of trade.

'Later, m'boy, later,' said Uncle Piggott, breaking off the low conversation he had been having with a turbaned man dressed in ornate livery. 'You're in luck. I'm told that Babu Dutt has had business to conduct with Rajah Ram Mohan Roy, and if we can wait a few minutes, we may join them for tea.'

'A king?' asked Griffith.

'Not really our sort of king,' Uncle Piggott smiled. 'Think of him as a prince.'

Henrietta smoothed her gown, creased from the carriage ride.

They were led up the stairs and into a large room overlooking the gardens. Henrietta had expected to marvel at rich oriental tapestries. Instead, oil paintings hung from every available space on the walls and displayed scenes of the English countryside, men in red riding coats blowing horns in the hunt, vases blooming with roses, and bowls dripping with grapes.

'Babu Dutt is a lover of all things European,' her uncle said, following her gaze.

Close up, Henrietta saw that the lacquer finish on some of the paintings was cracked, and flakes of paint were lifting in the humidity.

There were marble fireplaces on three sides of the room, their mantelpieces bearing silver ornaments in the shapes of countless Grecian gods and goddesses. High above hung cut-crystal chandeliers, glinting in the light shafting through the French windows. The clutter of furniture was mainly European in style, dark-wooded with heavy fabric. However, in the centre of the room were two divans, circular in shape so that people could sit all the way around, facing out into the room. They were so low to the ground as to require those seated to be almost sitting cross-legged. Uncle Piggott indicated that they should sit in the chairs closest to the divans.

'Cat got your tongue, Henrietta?' asked her uncle. 'Unlike you to be so quiet.'

Henrietta collected her thoughts. 'What shall I call the Rajah? Your highness? Or …?'

'You need say nothing at all. In fact, it would probably be better not to. If you're asked a question, look shy. You can look shy, can't you?'

She fought back a smile and cast her eyes to her hands, clasped in her lap.

'Ha, well that's a start. Though, I can't say as how it suits you.' He looked at her fidgeting brother and sighed. 'Just do your best, Griffith.'

There was a flurry of servants, and Henrietta, Griffith and Uncle Piggot rose to their feet as the *babu* ushered in his guest of honour and made the introductions. Babu Dutt's appearance was strange, with his odd combination of Indian *dhoti* draped about his legs and his English topcoat. He made a great fuss of Henrietta and Griffith and radiated the same genial warmth as her uncle.

'You are as lovely as your uncle told me, Miss Burbridge,' he said, bowing. 'And about the same age as my own dear daughter, Amrita. She is to be married soon. It will be a wonderful ceremony, you should come.'

Henrietta was taken aback at the sudden familiarity, but Uncle Piggott was nodding and smiling so she did likewise.

The sense of ease that had stolen over her as Babu Dutt talked disappeared on being introduced to the Rajah. His expression was stern, and he wore the most unusual turban she had yet seen: brightly coloured and wound into a flat hat under which black curls bushed out about his ears. He was a handsome man, with strong regular features and a striking moustache, but he was rather old—almost as old as her father, she judged, at least forty.

As tea was served, the men discussed trade matters and politics. Henrietta sipped her tea, sneaking occasional looks at the Rajah.

'The last three years have been the worst we've ever had,' Uncle Piggott expounded. 'Whatever possessed the government to limit the new Charter, still astounds me.'

'And do you think Amherst will succeed in improving the situation in Canton?' Babu Dutt asked deferentially.

'Not a chance, not a chance. The Chinese denied us access twenty years ago. They've turned down the Dutch and the Russians. They're not about to change their mind now, are they?'

Henrietta noticed that the Rajah remained quiet through most of their talk. She'd spent her childhood listening to animated talk among men about the wrongs and rights of governmental decisions. Her father was often congratulated on his eldest daughter's perspicacity, and she attributed that to her ability to look like she was listening. None of the talk changed anything, though. Perhaps the Rajah thought so too. He did look very intelligent as he listened.

'Master Griffith might like to show his sister the aviaries?' Babu Dutt was smiling sympathetically at Griffith who had controlled his fidgets by dint of wrapping his ankles around the legs of his chair.

Henrietta understood the signal. Time for the men to get down to business. She rose and, on impulse, curtsied.

Later in the carriage on the way home, Uncle Piggott said, 'Perhaps you should consider getting used to remaining silent, young lady. You made quite an impression on the Rajah.'

No downcast eyes now. 'Why, what did he say?'

'He said you were the loveliest *houri* he had ever seen.'

She hoped it was a compliment.

'Have you two finished writing your letters home?' asked Aunt Piggott.

She asked that every morning and, since Henrietta and Griffith were poor correspondents, they rarely answered in the affirmative.

Rose and Beth wrote long letters addressed to both Griffith and herself. Rose invariably made thinly veiled allusions to the military. Beth often included one of her drawings. Her brother Bill rarely put pen to paper, although Rose dutifully told them that he hoped they were having a good time. Of course, Papa was too busy to write himself. *Dearest Henrietta*, Mama would write before passing on her father's admonitions to be on her best behaviour, adding her own addendum that Henrietta wasn't to ride astride, on any account.

Henrietta's favourite letters were from her cousin Eliza. Letters from Eliza had turned out to be an unanticipated benefit of moving to Calcutta since, although the two families were still estranged, Eliza was free to write and Henrietta was able to receive her letters without parental strictures.

Eliza was entertaining in her reports of Mr Babcock's latest attentions to various young ladies of their acquaintance. Eliza herself seemed to be attracting some interest, Henrietta gleaned from the number of names of young gentlemen who were included in the family's picnic parties. She answered Eliza's letters promptly, but she preferred to write to her in the privacy of her room rather than under the eye of her aunt.

From Aunt Piggott's tone today, however, it looked as though writing home would replace Griffith and Henrietta's planned game of *écarté*. Henrietta could still beat him, but Griffith was beginning to play more strategically and so, with success in sight, he took every opportunity to try to recoup his losses.

Griffith scratched the words, *Dear Papa*.

Henrietta knew what he was writing about. The seed of the idea for a naval career had been planted on their voyage to India and had been germinating. Griffith had asked Uncle Piggott about it, but he'd said, 'business only seems dull from the outside' and 'you'll soon get used to it' and, when pressed, 'it's a matter for your father, m'boy'.

She stared at the blank page. She couldn't think of a thing to write to anyone. No one at home evinced much interest in matters outside New South Wales. It was hot, she would write. But then, they'd write that it had been hot there too. The humidity was oppressive. So it was there. The Hugli River stank with sewage and floating carcasses. But in Sydney, the Tank Stream had become so choked as to almost cease flowing. The natives of India were more civilised than she had expected, she wrote, and she tried to describe Babu Dutt's house. But back home, her sister would tell her, the governor had presented a medal to an elderly native, naming him Chief of the Broken Bay tribe, for his good influence on his fellows.

What she couldn't understand was why her mother showed so little interest in her news about India. Henrietta had expected her to attend avidly to every word, to ask questions, to delight in hearing about the governor-general's ball.

Aunt Piggott looked up from her book. 'Nothing to say, Henrietta?' she asked. 'How unusual.'

Henrietta bent her head and inscribed a few more words about her dancing lessons. It would have to do. She blotted the ink, more through habit than necessity, as the fan wafted gentle warm eddies over where she was seated.

'Two pages.' Her aunt sniffed. 'How disappointing for your dear mother. I'm sure she is most interested to learn all about India from you.'

'She knows a lot about India already,' said Henrietta, nettled. So much, she thought, that she doesn't want to know any more.

Aunt Piggott tilted her head sceptically. 'You do know that my dear sister was only five when she left Calcutta, don't you?'

'Yes, yes, of course,' stammered Henrietta. 'Mama was sent home to school in England, and Baroness Imhoff, that is to say, Mrs Hastings, gave her a beautiful red shawl and—'

'Yes, that old story. But five years old, all the same. About the same age as you were when your father insisted on uprooting you all to the ends of the earth. How much do you recall of England?'

Henrietta was about to protest that she had been six and certainly she remembered a lot about their home in Kent but, in truth, she wasn't sure how much of what she remembered was from her own experience or imagined, based on the tales of her mother.

Aunt Piggott didn't wait for a reply. 'Five years old — the same age as your grandmother when she was brought to India. Our mother barely remembered a thing about England when she and my father returned there.' The corners of her mouth twitched smugly, 'I spent my first fourteen years in India, of course. That's when I first knew Mr Martin, you know.'

Griffith blew loudly over the surface of his paper. His quill needed sharpening and large blobs of ink had pooled on the downstrokes of his letters. 'Finished,' he said with satisfaction. 'Cards, Henrietta?'

'Your uncle is expecting you to join him at Palmers, Griffith,' Aunt Piggott reminded him. 'Mind you hurry along. No dawdling along the way.'

Henrietta made to follow Griffith out of the room but her aunt forestalled her.

'And some practise at the pianoforte, for you, I think,' Aunt Piggott said.

Henrietta enjoyed playing and willingly practised for part of nearly every day, so it was tiresome to be told to do so. She vented her vexation with a heavy touch on the keys in imitation of Miss Desacourt, and she had the satisfaction of seeing her aunt wince. But after the first few bars, the pleasure of playing took over until she almost forgot her aunt was still in the room.

After some time, her aunt put her book aside. 'I ran into an acquaintance of yours yesterday while I was out,' she said languidly.

Henrietta stopped playing. It was so like Aunt Piggott to decide to speak when she'd become immersed in the piece.

'Mrs Nairne, she is now,' Aunt Piggott added.

Henrietta waited for more; however, as nothing more was forthcoming, she asked, 'How is Mrs Nairne?'

Her aunt disregarded the question. 'She was a Miss Burton when I knew her, of course.' Her hand lingered over the bonbons in the bowl by her side. 'At school with your mother, though I suppose you knew that.' She selected a pink one. 'Came to stay at Barrow House with us one summer.' She took a hesitant nibble. 'Can't say I thought much of her.' She pursed her lips in distaste and put the sweet back on the plate and wiped the tips of her fingers with her handkerchief. 'Very fond of quoting from the Bible, I remember. Much too much a Wesleyan for my tastes.'

With no more forthcoming, Henrietta recommenced playing. She'd got as far as the next bar when her aunt spoke again.

'She's off back home to England now that the regiment has been recalled. She was very full of herself about it. Asked if I wanted her to take any messages back—very impudent of her—it's not as if we moved in the same circles.'

Henrietta raised her hands over the keyboard again.

'She asked to be remembered to you, of course.'

Henrietta let her hands fall to her lap. 'That was most thoughtful of her.'

'Seemed to think you had some kind of infatuation with one of her husband's officers.' Her aunt picked up another bonbon.

'Captain Cowin,' Henrietta said his name without thinking. She wished she could have bitten the words back. It was bad enough to know that her aunt had been gossiping about her, but worse to have let slip that the story was true.

'Yes, that was the name, I think.' Aunt Piggott took a large bite this time.

Henrietta waited. It was a long time since she'd seen Captain Cowin. It was another world then; a world where a look was enough for you to think you understood a man's heart, and a word from him was all the assurance you needed that his feelings were in sympathy.

Her aunt chewed thoughtfully until, finished, she took a sip of tea before speaking. 'Kandy, that was the name of the place. Captain Nairne and your young fellow were at the battle at Kandy. Nasty business. Captain Nairne was lucky indeed to survive.' With only pink bonbons remaining, and her tea finished, Aunt Piggott rose. 'Well, enough idle chat, Henrietta. The little ones will have finished their nap by now.' She rose to leave.

'And Captain Cowin?'

'Oh, he died.'

Henrietta knew that these were the words her aunt would say even before she spoke them. It wasn't as though she had known him well, she reflected, not really. But the thought that he had been alive and now wasn't, was incomprehensible. Thousands of men died at Kandy, she knew. He was just one. But he was the one she knew.

'I thought you were meant to be practising,' said her aunt. She walked to the door. 'Oh, and Mr Martin has asked if he might be permitted to pay his attentions.' She paused. 'We wrote to your parents and they have agreed.'

Chapter 11

As rich as Croesus

'But what would you do, Caroline?' Henrietta asked yet again. 'He calls at the house every day. Now that Griffith has gone off to join the Navy, I thought I'd get to spend more time with Uncle Piggott, but Aunt won't let me go with him, just in case I miss Mr Martin's visit. And, whenever he's there, she keeps *popping out to check on the babies*, leaving me alone with him.'

Caroline was lounging on the divan in a spectacularly unladylike fashion—one stockinged leg hooked over the back, the other dangling from the side. Her mother had left to make her calls, otherwise Caroline would never have dared. Since Caroline's brother Teddy had left for England, Henrietta had become a frequent visitor to the house. According to Caroline, they weren't allowed to ask her to visit before, as their mother considered Henrietta to be an 'unnecessary distraction' to her son. Since Henrietta had absolutely no romantic interest in Teddy, she thought it a pity that Mrs Walker had wasted all their time for no good purpose.

'And he spends the whole visit asking about my health and then telling me all about his aches and pains. And he smells. You know, that old smell.'

But Caroline replied, 'Well, since he hasn't actually proposed, you don't need to be worrying about it, do you? What I want to know is how Patrick is going in your uncle's business? I've quizzed him about it but, you know Patrick, he just smiles and charms me onto another topic.'

'All right, I suppose,' Henrietta replied doubtfully. 'He says Uncle Piggott doesn't give him very much responsibility, so it's hard for him to prove himself. There was a lost consignment a while ago, apparently. The whole thing caused a bit of a fuss.'

'He told me about that. Just a mix-up, you know what the natives are like. Pilfered, no doubt.'

'Why are you so interested?' Henrietta was startled to hear that Patrick would confide such a thing in someone outside the family.

'Oh, no reason, really.' Caroline swung her legs back around to sit upright. 'Oh, all right then. Mama says that she doesn't want to see me talking with him, or anyone else that matter, unless they own their own business or, at the very least, have a partnership.' She pouted. 'I don't see what the fuss is all about. We're wealthy ourselves. I can't see that I have to marry into money.' She sighed theatrically. 'There's no limit to the woman's avarice.'

They both got the giggles.

Wiping the tears from her eyes, Henrietta, still trying to catch her breath, said, 'You could marry a Rajah and even then ...'

'It still wouldn't be enough to satisfy Mother's base desires,' finished Caroline, and they both collapsed, howling with laughter again.

Several deep breaths later, Henrietta had calmed down enough to ask something she'd been too abashed to ask anyone else. 'You know Rajah Ram Mohan Roy—'

'Not personally,' interrupted Caroline through her hiccoughs.

'No, seriously—he said, or Uncle Piggott said that he—' She took another breath. 'He said I was the loveliest *houri* he'd ever seen.'

'Did he?' Caroline looked at her appraisingly. 'Well, you are very ...'

'I'm not pretty,' said Henrietta. 'I'm not delicate like you, or like my sisters. Rose's very pretty, and everyone says that Beth's features are the sweetest they've ever seen.'

'No, not pretty,' said Caroline slowly, 'you're more ... statuesque.'

'Like a statue?' Henrietta objected.

'No, no. But you're tall, and your features are strong, and men look at you, you know they do.'

'So, then, what's a *houri*?'

'It does sound rather risqué, doesn't it?' Caroline said with a laugh. 'It means a young *virgin*, that's all.

It's in their religion, I think. Something about companions of the faithful in heaven.'

'Oh.'

'Though, if Mr Martin gets round to proposing ...'

Henrietta threw a cushion at her.

It turned out that Babu Dutt's invitation to his daughter's wedding had been made in all seriousness. Uncle Piggott told her that Hindu weddings ran over days, but they would only be attending part of the ceremony for the exchange of vows.

Although Henrietta assumed she would be sitting with her uncle and Patrick, immediately on their arrival at Babu Dutt's house, she was whisked away by the other female guests. Their rich silk saris rustled about her and the bangles on their arms clinked and glittered on arms and hands, which were painted with henna in ornate designs. They fussed over her and introductions were made to numerous relatives, but her meagre Hindustani collapsed amid the bustle and she lost track of which were sisters of the bride and which were friends.

The smell from the oil lamps hung heavy in the windowless room, and her head was pounding; however, there was no sign that any of the ladies would be leaving anytime soon. If Griffith had been there, or even Cousin Arthur, she would at least have someone to talk with. Cousin Arthur had left to go back to school in England, and she'd barely seen Griffith since he'd joined the Navy. Griffith's letters were making her miss him more. He was regretting his choice bitterly; in each letter, he sounded more and more miserable.

Finally, when noise from the bridegroom's procession could be heard, the women all rushed out to welcome him, Henrietta in tow. A continuous cacophony of horns and bells assailed her. The shouts from those in the procession matched the cheers of the onlookers who gathered outside the gates. The bridegroom was seated on a white stallion and, against the glare of the setting sun, his coat was haloed in glinting jewels.

Through the crowd, Uncle Piggott and Patrick fought their way to join her.

'Looks pretty cheerful about his last moments of freedom, doesn't he?' joked Patrick under cover of the noise.

'Now, now, m'boy,' replied Uncle Piggott. 'There comes a time when every chap needs to settle down. Even you, I dare say, might come to it one day.'

'He's young, isn't he?' Henrietta said to her uncle. The groom's beauty was untouched by time. She estimated his age as not much more than her own. She wondered how he could afford to marry.

'Son of Babu Mullick—that old chap over there,' her uncle answered by way of explanation.

A large feather brushed past her cheek, quickly followed by the rest of the elaborate ornamentation on Lady Caldwell's hat.

'The father is as rich as Croesus,' Lady Caldwell hissed, leaning close, 'but not long for this world, I hear. The son is going to be a rich man indeed.'

Henrietta glanced about, worried that other guests might hear. However, the Indian women had broken into peels of high-pitched ululation, which masked Lady Caldwell's comments.

'Good-looking chap, isn't he?' Lady Caldwell continued. 'I wonder what he'll think of his young bride.'

'He hasn't seen her?' Henrietta asked.

'No, no. She's a proper young lady.' Lady Caldwell's eyes flicked sharply between Henrietta and Patrick, as if to imply, *unlike some.*

Inside, chairs had been provided in deference to the European guests, but these were pushed against the walls and left vacated by all but the elderly and most sedentary. Lady Caldwell and Miss Prendergast looked as though they were attempting to close their nostrils without using their hands.

At every opportunity, the guests moved to mill about the bridal couple, arranging their robes and adjusting the garlands of flowers that were strung about their necks. Henrietta followed suit, awkwardly at first since it seemed an oddly disrespectful thing to do at a wedding, but she was keen to escape the whispering crones.

Taller than most of the women in front of her, Henrietta could easily watch Amrita, Babu Dutt's young daughter, as she stepped to the groom's side and they began to circle the flame burning in a bowl. The couple started to recite together, but Henrietta could only understand the beginnings of each phrase, '*I am ...*', '*I am ...*'. Their stepping chant stayed in her mind, soothing and calming her headache. At first, she thought they might be taking their vows but that appeared to happen later when she caught the Hindustani words that meant *house, children, husband, wife*.

With a burst of laughter and talk, the ceremony was over. Babu Dutt made his way around all his guests, bowing and shaking hands with enthusiasm.

'So glad you were able to come, Miss Burbridge. A Hindu wedding is not something to be missed, I am thinking. You will not have been seeing anything of the sort back in New South Wales.'

'Indeed no, Babu Dutt,' said Henrietta. 'It was all so beautiful. I am most grateful for your invitation.'

'Not at all, not at all. Perhaps your uncle will soon be inviting me to your wedding.' And then, after a warning look from Uncle Piggott, he said, 'Well, as soon as may be. Though marriage is a good thing for the young.' He smiled broadly.

'Yes, indeed,' said Uncle Piggott jovially. 'Keeps them on the straight and narrow, I always say.'

Babu Dutt passed on to talk with other guests, and her uncle said, 'Well, that's that. Duty done. Supper's waiting back at Hastings Street.' He patted his belly. 'Won't get much here. This lot ...' he said, waving waved his hand in the direction of the Indian guests, 'will get a feast when they move on to the bridegroom's house, but Babu Mullick hasn't invited us. How about it, are you coming?'

Henrietta, now alert and interested, opted to stay a little longer with Patrick. So once her uncle left, she and Patrick continued to take in the festivities. By this time, trays of food were passed about offering delicacies.

'Uncle Piggott wasn't wrong. Not much in the way of real food,' said Patrick, disappointed.

Then more servants appeared carrying massive trays that required two bearers each. The trays were covered with red cloth, richly brocaded with gold, and heaped with jewels of every description and colour—rubies, pearls, emeralds, and sapphires of bright yellow and blue. The admiration of the guests was enthusiastic, and Henrietta realised she was seeing Amrita's dowry. Babu Dutt's beam of pleasure grew with every sigh that accompanied the display of each successive tray.

Henrietta remembered her uncle saying that Babu Dutt was wealthy, but she had no conception before of the extent of his riches. Amrita had three older sisters, she knew, and he must have also provided such gifts upon their marriages. So then, if the groom's father, Babu Mullick, was considered wealthier than Babu Dutt, he must be very rich indeed. Unbidden, the image of Mr Martin swam before her and she remembered Lady Caldwell's whisper, '£1,000,000 sterling, Sir James tells me'. Was Mr Martin 'as rich as Croesus'? She gazed at the young groom, who was staring with adoration at his new wife.

She pictured Mr Martin and herself seated upon cushions, looking in each other's eyes. Mr Martin's legs were crossed painfully and he rubbed his wrinkled hands over his knobbly knees. Gazing into her eyes, he said, 'I hope your dowry included some of that goanna oil you were telling me about for my rheumatism, m'dear. I'll need you to rub some into these old knees of mine later tonight, dear one.'

She shook her head sharply to rid herself of the picture, but the worry remained.

When she'd tried to talk with Caroline about Mr Martin, she'd dismissed the problem since, as Mr Martin hadn't actually proposed yet, Henrietta needn't make a decision. But his visits to Hastings Street were becoming increasingly frequent and he'd taken to asking her to walk with him about the garden, which meant that Aunt Piggott's excuses to leave them alone together were mounting. What would she do if he did ask her? Her eyes roved across the trays of jewels.

Patrick must have been looking at them too for he murmured to himself, 'Freedom has a price then, I suppose.'

She thought it would be wonderful to be rich. She could do as she liked. If she wanted to travel anywhere, she could go in her own ship. She wouldn't need to wait for others to go to exotic places. She could wear the best of everything, and her mother's red scarf would be relegated to everyday instead of best. She wished there were a rich man, who was young and preferably handsome, paying court to her. But young rich men could take their pick and, as Aunt Piggott missed no opportunity to point out, the daughter of a farmer from Botany Bay was no prize, regardless of how important such a personage might be in the limited society of penal settlement.

And what if she did refuse Mr Martin? Would her invitation to live with the Piggotts expire? After all, they would have done their best for her education. She'd be sent back to live with her family, sharing a room with her sisters. She could almost hear Rose's taunt, 'what, dreams didn't come true, then?' Her mother would be disapproving and—the thought struck her with horror—expect her to consider some man like Mr Babcock, or worse. And her father? She saw herself standing outside his study door, hand raised to knock.

Her hands balled into fists in her lap.

'Ready to escape?' asked Patrick in a low voice. 'This'll go on for a while yet and I'm starving.'

She accepted with relief. She couldn't bear to look at the beautiful couple any longer.

Excuses made and expressions of gratitude complete, she joined Patrick in the marble colonnade. They both still wore the garlands of flowers that had been thrown about their necks as they left. In the night air, the fragrance of the flowers was all honey and passionfruit.

'Mr Piggott has taken the carriage,' he said. 'I'll sort something out for us.' He snapped his fingers and the tall turbaned servant she'd seen on her first visit materialised.

She sauntered a few steps while they waited, and Patrick walked with her. The rhythm of their steps reminded her of the ceremony.

'Did you know what they were chanting as they walked around the fire together?'

'My Hindustani lessons were mainly for matters of business,' he said, 'but old Bruxton, the chap who taught me, made me memorise all sorts of Hindu rituals. Said it would broaden my mind. This one is a fine piece. Here's the English version.' He began to chant quietly, 'I am the sky; you are the earth. I am the thought; you are the speech. I am the fire and you are the fuel. I am the song; you are the verse. I am the ocean; you are the shore. I am the strength but you are the beauty. I am—' He broke off as the turbaned servant approached again.

Henrietta stared at him as he spoke with the man. She hadn't thought Patrick was a romantic sort of man. Here was the solution to the puzzle of Caroline's continuing interest in him, despite his lack of money. If he had more of that kind of poetry to recite then no wonder he'd earned his reputation as a ladies' man.

Negotiations over, the turbaned servant beckoned and four bearers approached with a palanquin.

Henrietta looked doubtfully at the single palanquin at the bottom of the steps.

'More fun with two,' suggested Patrick.

'Not entirely ladylike,' she said, trying to sound arch.

'Come on. Where's your sense of adventure?'

Trying not to think of what her aunt would say, Henrietta climbed in and Patrick squeezed in beside her, his arm draped loosely about her shoulders so they could fit. With a lurch, the palanquin was raised and began to move. Thinking to avoid being recognised, Henrietta flicked the curtains shut on her side and, and following her lead, Patrick did likewise.

'Nice and cosy,' he said with a grin. 'You can be as unladylike as you please and no one will be the wiser.'

She stuck out her tongue at him.

'Not such a lady then,' he teased.

As it turned out, the ride was more comfortable than usual. They were so compacted as to make any sliding impossible. And he was right, she thought, it was fun with each sway and bump more hilarious than the last. It was like being with Griffith again.

They were still laughing as they made their way into the house. However, they then fell quiet, both struck by the impropriety of their late entrance.

The entrance hall was dimly lit with just one lamp by the large mirror. It seemed that no one had heard their arrival.

'Look at you, with your flowers.' She reached up to the garland around his neck, its blooms now bruised after being jostled against her in the palanquin.

'I'd quite forgotten I was wearing them. We've grown quite attached,' he said, adding, 'I think I shall always wear flowers in future.'

Henrietta went to draw her own garland over her head but it snagged on the pins of the ribbon in her hair. 'I'm quite caught up,' she said with a giggle. 'Look where your adventure has led.' She tugged at the ribbon.

'Here, let me.' Patrick deftly twisted the garland loose.

At that moment, Aunt Piggott appeared, three servants by her side bearing lamps. She stood for a long moment, speechless. Finally, she said in a controlled tone, 'Home at last, I see. Lakshmi can bring your supper to your room, Henrietta.'

Henrietta didn't dare look at Patrick as she followed Lakshmi's lamp down the hall. She glimpsed her reflection in the mirror as she passed. Her face was flushed, her eyes large and bright, her tangled hair crackling in the glow of the lamp.

Following the palanquin ride with Patrick, she learnt that Aunt Piggott and her mother had more in common than she'd thought. By way of punishment, Aunt Piggott restricted Henrietta's social outings.

Patrick, too, had his wings clipped. Uncle Piggott sent him on errands that took him up the river for days at a time. When he was at Hastings Street, he left for the Writers' Building early each day. He no longer dropped by the house as he went about the town on business. On those occasions when he joined them for dinner, he maintained an air of manly gravity, completely different from his usual banter.

Henrietta did still get to see Caroline, but only at dancing lessons and, even there, the atmosphere had changed. It was nothing to do with her own troubles, she was sure, but Caroline skipped from topic to topic, rarely attending long enough to do more than fulfil the surface obligations of conversation.

The monsoon season had arrived and the oppressive humidity blanketed her wits and rendered the slightest movement effortful. Most days, she sought refuge on the screened verandah overlooking the garden.

She fingered the thick package of letters that lay on her lap. She turned them over, running her fingers across each surface, delaying opening them for as long as she could. One letter, much folded and overwritten crossways, was from Eliza. Her impulse was to indulge in the pleasure of reading it first. However, the other letter she knew to be from her parents, and it was sure to be unpleasant reading. Aunt Piggott would have reported all her goings on. Bad medicine first, she decided.

The letter from her mother was—as anticipated— filled with admonitions: 'What were you thinking? Were you thinking at all? What if someone had seen you?' Her mother was also at pains to point out that 'suitable suitors might be lost by such injudicious behaviour and the formation of an inappropriate relationship'. Although she didn't name him, Henrietta understood that the 'suitable suitor' in question was, without a doubt, Mr Martin. And, of course, late-night palanquin riding with a young man might be considered 'injudicious'. But, what did she mean: 'inappropriate relationship'? She didn't mean Patrick, surely?

Henrietta read through that part of her mother's letter again: 'don't know what your aunt and uncle must be thinking, a young man as chaperone, indeed'. Henrietta nearly laughed out loud. Patrick, of all people. For Caroline, perhaps—though even there, she thought Patrick's hopes unduly sanguine.

Her mood darkened again as she read the postscript added by her father: the words 'disappointment, both you and Griffith throwing away opportunity, bring you and Griffith back home' leapt from the page. Tears smarted and she looked up from the letter to steady herself.

Rain began to fall, drumming against the leaves of her aunt's precious rose bushes, shattering the petals. What had Griffith done? She'd had no word from him for weeks. She'd hoped his sudden silence after weeks of miserable letters meant that he'd settled into Navy life, but apparently not, by her father's tone.

Through the sheeting rain, the black top of a carriage made its way along the street beyond the wall. *Not now,* she thought, *Mr Martin can't be thinking of visiting now.* Most people delayed their visits until the late afternoon at this time of the year, in the brief interval after the humidity had spent itself in the downpour and before the heat began to lift the water back into the air. She glanced down at the letters still on her lap. She wouldn't have time to read Eliza's letter properly, so she felt she should wait. But she couldn't wait; she needed a dose of Eliza's gossip to clear her mind if she had to talk with Mr Martin.

She scanned the tight script: the first words she saw were 'proposal of marriage'. Not Eliza, surely not Eliza. Eliza was younger—only by five months, it was true, but younger all the same. She read on, hurrying as she could hear voices marking Mr Martin's arrival in the entrance hall. Dr Forster had proposed to Eliza and, yes, he was a lot older, though she wrote, 'not as old as your Mr Martin'. Dr Forster was only seventeen years older, at thirty-five years of age.

Lakshmi entered the room so silently that Henrietta hadn't realised she was there. 'Yes?' she said, distractedly still perusing Eliza's letter.

'Mr Martin asks if you might be at home, Miss Burbridge.'

It took a moment for her to think what to do. 'Yes, yes, I suppose,' she answered. 'Show him in. Oh, and please see if my aunt will be joining us.' She didn't really want to see her aunt—she was tired of fending off her disapprobation—but she didn't want to spend time alone with Mr Martin either.

He must have been waiting outside the door. She was still refolding the letter when he joined her.

As they exchanged empty pleasantries, Henrietta's mind was elsewhere. When she finally remembered to suggest he might like to sit down, Mr Martin did so gratefully, emitting a barely suppressed groan as he completed his descent.

He cleared his throat as if to speak but then, baulking, remained silent.

Henrietta filled the pause, saying, 'I hope you are keeping well, Mr Martin?' Silently, she berated herself for the question. Mr Martin needed no encouragement to talk about his health or lack of it.

However, Mr Martin replied, 'Fine, fine, m'dear. Most fine in fact.' He paused again. 'So fine, that is to say,' he said, stumbling on, 'that your dear aunt and uncle have encouraged me to, to—'

Alarmed, Henrietta looked to the door, willing her aunt to come.

Mr Martin took a deep breath. 'You'd think at my time of life, these things might come a little easier but, alas, they do not. Let's say, that the time has come, the time has come for—well, some might say the time has indeed very well come—for me to take, to take a wife.'

Henrietta stared at him mutely. She'd known it might come to this. Of course, she'd known. But the knowing and the event itself were two completely different things. Hysteria welled up; she didn't trust herself to speak.

Mr Martin was looking at her in consternation. 'Are you well, m'dear? I know this must come as a shock. After all, you are such an innocent young thing that, no doubt, such thoughts may not have crossed your mind. Why, you have gone pale. You're not going to faint, are you?' He flapped his hands futilely and then stood to ring for Lakshmi.

'Miss Burbridge has been taken ill,' he said rapidly when Lakshmi entered. He went to crouch beside Henrietta's chair but his arthritis prevented him from doing more than a slight bow. 'I'll let you get used to the idea, shall I? Have a talk with your aunt, that'll be the ticket. We have lots of time, lots of time, though of course, more time for you than for me, but still, plenty of time. How we shall laugh about this day in the years to come, you and I.' He gave a little chuckle in anticipation and took his leave.

Chapter 12

All the felicity

She should have refused Mr Martin on the spot, of course. She knew that now. If she'd had the presence of mind to simply thank him and give some excuse, then she would at least have had some way to manage what was occurring now. She'd thought of numerous excuses, when she'd had the long sleepless dark to mull over them.

She might have said that her parents did not wish her to marry until she was older—eighteen, at least. Three years would be so long to wait that Mr Martin could withdraw his offer without losing face. After all, he had said he was in a hurry to marry. She might have said that she had been made another offer; that she had an understanding with a beau back in New South Wales, and they couldn't make it public because they were both so young. Even her aunt and uncle didn't know about it, so could he please avoid mentioning it to them.

But it was all very well thinking of excuses now, when Aunt Piggott was taking every opportunity to remind her of her limited prospects—'your father's wealth is locked up in land, there may be lots of it, but it's all worthless saltpans, as I understand it'. It was

Henrietta's 'duty to her family to marry well'. And, with her complexion—'I told you to use the lemon and vinegar poultice'—she couldn't expect to be married for her looks.

Uncle Piggott hadn't said anything to her directly, but he had talked at length one evening of the wisdom of Babu Dutt's daughter in complying with her father's wishes to marry Babu Mullick's son, since in a matter of months, the old *babu* had died and young Amrita was married to the wealthiest *babu* in India. Her uncle had taken to muttering, as if to himself, 'old men can't last forever', and 'fine old fellow that Mr Martin' and 'good head for business, that Mr Martin' whenever she chanced to be within earshot.

Mr Martin himself hadn't reappeared to press his suit, for which Henrietta was grateful. Instead, he'd written her a letter, restating his offer and his hopes. He would wait to hear from her uncle and aunt as to her answer. How long he would wait, she didn't know; however, she did know that she couldn't sustain her passive resistance for much longer. She had to refuse. She knew it in every fibre of her being. It was the consequence of that refusal that she feared. She knew her father too well to think that his threat that she would have to go home was made idly. She knew too that her mother, on her return, would exert the same pressure to marry well, regardless of suitor.

With no way out, she feared she must accept.

She spent the days that followed within the confines of the house. She longed to find out how Griffith was faring. Her father's mention of him in his letter was worrying her. Might he have done something reckless—deserted the Navy, perhaps? That would mean ruin. She couldn't imagine what life would be like for him back with the family under those circumstances.

Lakshmi was her sole companion. She'd taught Lakshmi to play cards but, as Lakshmi considered that her position meant she should always lose, this detracted from the challenge and reduced its power of distraction. She'd asked her uncle if she could go with him on his inspection visits to the new house and *godowns* he was building over the other side of the river in Shibpur, but he'd shook his head sadly.

The only time she was permitted to leave the house was to continue her dancing lessons. Once there, she could talk to Caroline, but only in snatches since Caroline was always surrounded by other giggling friends and had grown even more distant than before. Henrietta had begun to feel as she had done when she first arrived—isolated on the social rim. There were rarely any male partners to dance with these days, so they made do. Being among the tallest, Henrietta frequently took the male lead, which meant she was confused when she had to switch roles several times in succession.

When the dance mistress began to demonstrate the new steps for them, to the thudding pianoforte accompaniment of Miss Desacourt, Henrietta seized the opportunity to have a word with Caroline.

'So, he's done it now,' she whispered.

'Patrick? What's he done?' Caroline replied.

'Sorry? Patrick?' Henrietta was confused.

'Just because I told him …' She hesitated at the blank expression on Henrietta's face. 'Sorry, who are we talking about?'

'Mr Martin. Mr Martin proposed.'

'Oh that,' Caroline said dismissively. 'I knew he'd done that.'

'How could you know?' asked Henrietta, side-tracked.

'Your aunt told my mother, of course.' She paused, staring at the feet of their instructor. Then, as if remembering where she was in the conversation, she added, 'You'll be saying yes, of course.'

'No,' Henrietta said, perturbed, 'how could you think that? No, no, no, I cannot.'

'Why ever not?'

'Mr Martin.' Henrietta emphasised, since Caroline was missing the point. 'But if I refuse, I'm going to be sent home.'

The piano was struck with a final blow, the dance mistress finished her demonstration and everyone rose to take their places for their turn to practise the steps.

Since she hadn't watched a single step, Henrietta was at a loss. Her partner, a red-faced girl with eyes spaced so narrowly that to look at her made Henrietta cross-eyed, pushed her around the floor gesturing directions.

'Good, good. Some of you did well, very well indeed,' said the instructress. 'Others not so.'

Henrietta felt all eyes turn to her.

'You will all watch again. Come, Miss Snapcock, Miss Leighton. Show the others how it is done.' As they took the floor, the dance mistress accompanied the piano beat with heavy thumps of her staff.

Caroline stepped up beside Henrietta. 'Perhaps you could think of another suitor. You're quite fond of the military, aren't you? I'm sure there will be rich pickings at the Fort William concert. Ask Patrick to take you along.'

When she did ask Patrick, he responded so quickly in the negative that she thought her question had offended him in some way. However, a few days later, he caught up with her as she made her way out. Waving Lakshmi away, he drew her aside.

'Can you get out of your dancing lesson without being missed?' he asked urgently.

'Why?'

'I can take you to see Griffith, if you're game. Mr Piggott's asked me to take some urgent correspondence down to Diamond Harbour. HMS *Coromandel* is anchored not far down river. I could take you.'

As much as Henrietta was missing Griffith, she couldn't understand why Patrick was suggesting this, nor why he was intent on secrecy. 'But why?' she repeated.

'Neither of you want to go home, and I don't have any ideas.' His words tumbled out. 'Even if I did, I'm not the person who should be giving you advice, but Griffith is your brother and ...'

Henrietta wasn't at all sure Griffith would have any ideas that she hadn't thought about and already dismissed. However, she did want to see him. 'Is he on leave? Why isn't he coming here?'

'I ran into him when I was up at Barrackpore. He's meant to stay on board—punishment for some infraction or other—but apparently his captain will be on shore for a day or so, and the first mate is a friendly chap.'

Lakshmi was hovering by the door, nervously glancing in their direction.

Henrietta thought quickly. 'I'd have to show my face at dancing, but I could feign illness and ask to be excused to return home, perhaps?'

With that, the arrangements were made.

By mid-morning, subterfuge complete, Henrietta found herself at the *ghat* and being lifted into the pinnace. Patrick dismissed the men clustered about the boat and stood to pole it away from the steps himself. Henrietta caught a glimpse of Lakshmi's shawl disappearing in the direction of the markets further along the riverbank. No doubt, Lakshmi thought she could keep an eye out for her return from there just as easily as from the *ghat*. With a deft flick of the ropes, Patrick had the small sail catching the light breeze. He took his station by the rudder, the ropes looped about his hand.

'I had no idea that you were such a sailor.' She realised with a start that she knew little about him apart from his being born in Glasgow. They'd spent most of their time together in teasing.

'You're looking very comfortable there yourself,' he replied.

The waters of the Hugli were too fast flowing to be other than brown, but the morning light sparkled on the surface and Henrietta grinned with delight.

'But I'm no ocean sailor,' he continued. 'I had an uncle at Rothesay, so I did a lot of sailing around the Firth of Clyde as a lad.'

The river was busy, and Patrick stopped talking for a while to concentrate on avoiding the many small craft laden with goods for the markets and bobbing their way around the larger European vessels. The women congregated near parts of the bank where rough *ghats* had been fashioned by the placement of long flat rocks in wide steps down into the river. Their children, some clothed, some not, played in the shallows.

Henrietta watched as an older woman, thigh-deep in the water tossed the full length of a brightly coloured sari out across the surface like a lifeline, one hand keeping hold of its end. Then she slowly drew the cloth back towards her, agitating it with each pull. When all the fabric was back in her hands, she tossed it back out again and repeated the agitation. Her movements were smooth and rhythmic and mesmerising.

Once past the heaviest traffic, Patrick began to sing. He frequently sang to her piano accompaniment on those evenings he spent at Hastings Street but, here on the river where other voices might become lost in the air, his baritone was full and rich all the way through to the last verse.

'Come all ye maidens, young and old, pray come, be warned of me—Scots were never, never true, and Scots will never be.'

'I shall make sure to pass the message along to all my acquaintances,' Henrietta mocked, thinking of Caroline.

They were nearing the *Coromandel,* and Henrietta saw Griffith waiting by the rail. Two sailors stood by the winch.

'I can't stay,' Patrick said as they bumped alongside. 'Mr Piggott will have my head if I miss the mail packet. Griffith said he can get you back on dry land.'

Henrietta grasped the rope sling that was lowered. By the time she'd been hoisted aboard, the little pinnace had shot away.

Her cheeks were flushed and her hairpins were adrift, but her appearance seemed to please the men on board. The first mate, an older man with grizzled hair, insisted on leading her on a tour of the small vessel, leaving Griffith to trail in their wake. The two seamen who'd helped her on board managed to find work to keep themselves busy at any point where they stopped.

'And this here, Miss Burbridge, is the officers' quarters,' said her guide.

The men were all bent low to avoid knocking their heads on the beams above. Henrietta decided to take charge.

'I can't thank you enough for showing me around. I can see why my brother has such a high regard for you. However, unfortunately, my time is short, and my visit was prompted by the need to discuss urgent *family* matters.' She emphasised the word 'family', hoping that that would be sufficient to signal the need for privacy.

The first mate was flattered by her courtesy. 'Of course, of course. Here, you two.' He rounded on the seamen who had occupied themselves in moving some barrels from one position into another and then back again. 'Haven't you got something better to do? If you haven't, then I'll be finding you some.' With a wink to

Henrietta he herded the two men back up on deck, leaving Henrietta alone with Griffith at last.

'Do you know?' asked Griffith. 'About me leaving the Navy, I mean?'

'Father's furious, Griffith. He says he'll—'

'Get me sent home,' he said, finishing her sentence. 'And not me alone.'

'No. No, I'm to go too.' She sighed. 'We had high hopes, didn't we?' She felt old—far older than the girl who had dreamed of a soldier's love.

'Why can't you marry that old chap and be done with it?'

'Why can't you persist with the Navy?'

They looked at each other in silence. He was thinner than the last time she'd seen him; his cheeks were drawn and he had a grey pallor at odds with a life in the open air.

'I don't know what to do, Henrietta.' He said the words so quietly, she could barely hear them.

'Have you asked Uncle Piggott?'

Griffith gave a bitter laugh before taking on their uncle's tone. 'You'll soon get used to it, m'boy.'

'Do you not like being at sea?' Henrietta couldn't imagine that was the problem.

'I love being at sea,' Griffith said softly. 'It's the way they ...' He shook his head.

Henrietta could see he wasn't going to say more. Their father might call Griffith spoilt, but he was no more spoilt than she—and nor was he a whiner.

'Uncle Piggott has ships of his own. Why couldn't he let you work on one of them?' The idea sprang into being as she spoke.

The thought took a moment to take hold.

'I can ask on your behalf,' she said. 'I'll convince him. You'd be an asset to the business. More of an asset on a ship than on land, I mean. And,' she said with a note of triumph, 'Papa can't object because, after all, he wanted you to become part of the business right from the start.'

Griffith shook his head. 'You are the most marvellous sister.' He gave her a sudden fierce hug. Pulling away, he added, 'But that won't help you. It's not like I can make the old man any younger for you. You'd still have to go back.'

Her brief elation ebbed. 'Not unless you happen to have run across a rich, young, eligible gentleman who would think a "Botany Bay flower" was something of a catch,' she said.

'What sort of flower?'

'Oh, never mind.'

Griffith hesitated and then said, 'I can think of someone who's young, and a gentleman, and eligible who'd be happy to marry you. But he's not rich. But he does think you're rather beautiful.'

'Sorry?' Henrietta couldn't follow what he was thinking. 'Are you talking about someone we know?'

'Well, Patrick. I mean Patrick.'

'Patrick?' Henrietta was astounded. 'Well, he's certainly not rich,' she said. 'And he thinks I'm beautiful? How do you know that? What sorts of things do you two talk about?' She was discomforted at the thought.

'He happened to mention it,' Griffith explained hurriedly. 'In passing, you know.'

She paced about the narrow space. Patrick was quite handsome—nothing remarkable, but tall with a manly physique. She enjoyed his company—second to Griffith, he was the person with whom she felt most at ease. He was a friend. Is a friend the person you should marry? It felt sensible to think so. Not romantic, of course, not like Emmeline and Godolphin, nor like the dreams and schemes that she and Caroline had laughingly concocted.

The thought of Caroline brought her up short. How would Caroline feel if Henrietta were to become betrothed to Patrick? She waited for the pang of guilt that she thought she ought to feel, but it didn't come. Instead, she felt a vague excitement, as if Caroline's interest in Patrick gave him some kind of additional sheen—the glamour of the forbidden. But she didn't have the attractions of a fortune such as Caroline. Would he think her beauty, if indeed he did think her beautiful, enough to marry?

He was certainly not rich, though. In fact, his only asset was the patronage of Uncle Piggott. However, she might say the same of herself. So then, would her aunt and uncle look kindly on such a marriage? And might their support be financial in nature? She couldn't imagine her aunt being supportive; however, Uncle Piggott had great affection for Patrick and, she thought, for herself.

Her mind turned to her parents. It wouldn't be a marriage that her mother would be proud to boast about in society. Though, if Uncle Piggott were to be supportive then perhaps her mother could manage to gloss over any deficiencies. And if Papa found that he bore no expense, then quite possibly he would be essentially indifferent as to who she married.

'You know, Griffith,' she said thoughtfully, 'you are quite marvellous yourself.'

All she had to do now was convince the Piggotts. And Patrick, of course.

The visit to Griffith provided much to think about. She decided against raising her idea about Griffith directly with Uncle Piggott, since he'd already declared his opposition to Griffith leaving the Navy. Instead, she thought she might recruit Aunt Piggott to his cause, if only she could think how to make her aunt think of the idea herself. She just had to find the right moment.

Aunt Piggott was looking through *The Times*, which had arrived by the latest London mail. She was a noisy reader—the sort of reader who liked to apprise those about them of their reaction to each item, regardless of others not being cognisant of its content.

'Oh, well, that's a shame,' she exclaimed.

Henrietta looked up from her embroidery. It was the same piece she had brought with her from Sydney, still unfinished. She'd found through experience that it was far less vexing to be interrupted when sewing than when trying to sustain her attention on her own reading. Her aunt subsided and resumed reading.

'Tsk, tsk. I could have told them that.' Her aunt shook her head.

Henrietta glanced up, waited, then completed her stitch.

Aunt Piggott turned her attention to the classified advertising. 'Oh, my, now that would be a treasure,' she said with a sigh.

'What is it?' Henrietta couldn't help asking.

'Oh, a trifle … ' Her aunt's voice trailed off. 'But if only …'

Henrietta suppressed a sigh of her own.

Aunt Piggott put the paper down and took a sip of her tea. 'I won't be able to trust Captain Murray with it, though,' she said as though Henrietta were privy to her prior thoughts.

'Is there something you want from London?' Henrietta guessed.

'A few small pieces. But they're from the best jeweller. Rundell and Bridge, you know. If only I could see them before I bought them ... But, I can't be going back home right now.' She patted her belly.

Henrietta stared. She hadn't realised her aunt's condition until now.

'Your uncle would let me buy them, of course.'

'I'm sure you could trust Captain Murray.' Henrietta and Griffith had been entrusted to the care of Captain Murray and his wife to come to Calcutta. She couldn't imagine anyone doubting his integrity.

'But the selection needs to be made with some taste, and as trustworthy as the good captain is ...' Aunt Piggott said with a sniff.

Henrietta's pulse quickened. Dare she? 'Griffith has a good eye for such things,' she said, as though to herself.

'Does he?' Her aunt looked doubtful. 'Unusual talent for a young man.'

'Oh yes,' Henrietta said, thinking frantically. 'Mama has some fine pieces and she always says that Griffith is the only one of us who can tell which are the most valuable in her collection.'

'Fine pieces, you say.' The doubt in her aunt's voice increased. 'Anyway, it's not as if he can go off gallivanting on private commissions when he's in the Navy.'

'It is a pity ...' Henrietta began again, leaving the thought unfinished in imitation of her aunt.

This time it was her aunt who had to interrogate. 'A pity, what?'

'Well, what Griffith really wants is to be on a merchant ship. The Navy is no place for a young man of any sensibility or refinement, after all.'

Aunt Piggott nodded but did not answer.

Henrietta let the conversation drop. The seed was planted—she didn't want to over-water it. She continued her embroidery, her stitching neater than usual. Her head was still bowed over her work when one of the servants slid into the room with a tray piled high with the morning's letters and cards.

As usual, it was Aunt Piggott who sorted through them, selecting the most important for her further perusal. 'Here's one for you,' she said, her tone full of syrup. 'From your Mr Martin.'

Henrietta reached out a leaden hand and slowly opened it. With her aunt's eyes resting on her, she knew she would have to read it now. She scanned the first few sentences: *'I regret ... I offer my most ... I wish you all the felicity ...'* Her hand trembled and it was hard to keep the letter still enough to read.

'What is it?' said her aunt.

Henrietta put the pages on her lap and, drawing a steadying breath, she read it through again, this time slowly. 'Mr Martin.' She swallowed, then started again. 'Mr Martin begs to withdraw.'

'What?' Aunt Piggott snatched the paper from Henrietta's lap. She read it through. 'This cannot be.' She read it again. 'This is your doing, my girl. If you'd only accepted him when he first asked. Mr Martin is not a man to be kept waiting.'

Henrietta kept her eyes averted. If she looked up, then Aunt Piggott would see her exultation. She was free—she didn't have to marry Mr Martin, or anyone, or at least not anyone right now. And she had not been the one to refuse. Surely her parents wouldn't insist on her returning now? Life could go on as before.

Aunt Piggott did not speak again. Finally, Henrietta could bear the silence no longer. She raised her head. Aunt Piggott had risen and was looking out the window, unseeing. Her eyes in the reflection were glazed with tears.

'Not a man to be kept waiting,' she said, her voice cracking. 'He wouldn't wait then, and he's not waiting now.'

Embarrassed, Henrietta picked up her embroidery but her hands still shook and she could do no more than stare at it. 'I don't need to go the Caldwell's tonight, do I?' Henrietta asked. Mr Martin would be sure to be there. She couldn't face him, not tonight, at least.

'There will be more talk if you're not there.'

'Mr Martin would be too much of a gentleman—'

'Perhaps. But the Walkers knew of the proposal. Why you confided in Caroline is beyond me.'

Henrietta wanted to snap back that it was her aunt who had told Mrs Walker first, but she knew she was on shaky ground given her own confidences. She rose slowly.

'And you'd better be thinking about packing your things.'

Henrietta gaped at her.

'You were not considered a prize before this. Why would you think that anyone will have you now? Not damaged goods, of course, but certainly discarded.'

Silently, Henrietta protested. But she knew the social truths as well as her aunt. She scrabbled to retrieve her sense of freedom, but it had slipped through the bars.

Chapter 13

Where jilted lovers come

Henrietta wanted to stay outside for as long as it took for the last rays to die, but Uncle Piggott insisted that they enter.

The Caldwells' residence was cramped with numerous small rooms, none of which could accommodate the pressure of the many visitors for the ball. However, this worked to Henrietta's advantage, since she was determined to contrive to be in a different room to Mr Martin whenever possible. Aunt Piggott had remained at home, as usual, but Henrietta was flanked by Uncle Piggott and Patrick. She expected them to wander off to their respective friends and acquaintances as was their wont, but they stayed by her side.

'Do you think we might settle in just one room, m'dear?' Uncle Piggott complained. 'These poor old feet aren't up to all this peregrination.'

'I don't think Mr Martin's here,' said Patrick. 'You needn't worry.'

It was the first time Patrick had made any reference to recent events. Neither had Uncle Piggott, although he'd given her hand a quick pat as they alighted from the carriage. She gathered both had been apprised of the situation and she was grateful for their discretion. She'd been on the verge of tears since the afternoon, and her fragility enraged her. She was glad to be free of Mr Martin's proposal, she told herself. But she knew her aunt's social acuity was well tuned. There would be consequences, and being compelled to return to Sydney was the most tangible of these.

She straightened to her full height. 'I'm not the least worried,' she declared. 'When he arrives, I shall make a point of greeting him.'

Uncle Piggott gave her hand another little pat. 'That's the spirit.' He eased himself down onto a chair. 'You two run along. By the sound of that fiddle, the dancing will be starting up any minute, I should think.'

Patrick took her elbow and steered her through the crowded rooms in the direction of the music. 'May I tempt you to the dance floor, Miss Burbridge?' he asked. His lips twitched at his mock formality. 'Dance card not too full yet, I hope?'

'I may have room for one more gentleman,' she said, matching the lightness of his tone. 'Though you'd better be careful. I do tend to rather casually toss them aside.'

As they danced their way through the set, Henrietta's mind settled and she found herself watching the grace of Patrick's movements, rhythmically caught by the flow of the music. They stayed together for the following few dances, and

Henrietta was aware of the raised eyebrows from the onlookers. They could stare all they like, she thought. She'd failed to meet one of society's expectations—she could breach them all.

The music finished and they wandered from the room in search of refreshment. All thoughts of Mr Martin had diminished to a small buzz in the back of her mind.

She turned from the laden supper table with her punch and found, with a start, that she was facing Lady Caldwell. 'Thank you so much for your hospitality, Lady Caldwell,' she said automatically. 'The ball is perfectly splendid.'

Lady Caldwell acknowledged the compliment with a thin smile. 'Yes, you do seem to be enjoying yourselves.' She nodded curtly at Patrick by way of acknowledgement.

Patrick drained his cup.

'And the punch, too,' Lady Caldwell added as Patrick reached for a second cup. 'What's that you say, my dear?' Lady Caldwell turned to Miss Prendergast who, until now, had been hidden behind her bulk.

'I was saying,' said Miss Prendergast, in her whispery voice, 'it was lovely to see Miss Burbridge. I had worried that she might not feel up to coming.'

Henrietta wondered if she could ignore the comment on the pretext of it being barely audible. But that would lead Lady Caldwell to repeat it, and Lady

Caldwell's voice would reach the furthermost corner of the crowded room. 'I'm well, Miss Prendergast,' she said. 'Thank you for your concern.'

Patrick grasped her arm in a tight grip. She wasn't sure if he was attempting to pull her away or to keep her there.

Mr Martin was approaching.

Caroline was one step behind, she saw with relief. Caroline always had the knack of saying the right thing to smooth over difficult situations.

'Miss Burbridge,' said Mr Martin, bowing in his old-fashioned way. His baldpate had achieved an even brighter lustre than when last Henrietta had seen it. 'Delighted to see you.'

'As am I, also,' said Henrietta, extending the tips of her fingers.

There was a heartbeat of a pause, and then Mr Martin turned to draw Caroline in to their little circle. 'And of course, you all know the charming Miss Walker.'

Caroline blushed.

'And why, pray, Mr Martin do you look so satisfied with yourself?' Lady Caldwell cackled.

Something in the way she said it, made Henrietta think Lady Caldwell knew the answer. Patrick's grip on her arm was so tight she almost cried out.

'You are as astute as ever, Lady Caldwell,' Mr Martin answered. 'I am pleased indeed to announce that Miss Walker here has consented to be my bride.'

Patrick recovered before Henrietta. He gave their congratulations and smoothly steered her to the verandah. Uncle Piggott was nowhere to be seen. He'd probably taken the carriage back to Hastings Street, she thought. She felt a rush of aching weariness.

Patrick walked with her to the far end where the bright moonlight was cutting through the bamboo screens.

'Welcome,' he said, imitating Mr Martin's low bow. 'Welcome to where jilted lovers come to salve their wounds.'

His speech was clear, but he swayed a fraction, and Henrietta wondered how much he had drunk before they'd arrived.

'I wasn't jilted,' she retorted. 'I hadn't decided.'

'You hadn't decided what to decide. But Mr Martin, he's a man who knows a thing or two about deciding. And he decided on Caroline, not you.'

'You really are quite drunk, aren't you?'

'Not as drunk as I'm going to be. Once I've dropped you back home, I'm off to drink some more. So, have you had enough humiliation? Do you want to go?'

'I don't want to go home. Not to Hastings Street. And not back to Sydney, either.'

He gave her a long look. 'Griffith told me that was on the cards.'

At the mention of Griffith's name, the memory of her visit out to his ship flooded her mind.

'You knew about Caroline's engagement.' The realisation grew as she spoke.

'What did I know? I didn't know anything about Mr Martin until tonight, I swear.'

'But you knew Caroline was no longer interested in you. Why else would you …?' *Why else would you make sure to have someone else in reserve?*

Patrick moved closer. He gently turned her face into the shafts of moonlight. 'Why else would I, what?'

'You told Griffith that you—that you think me beautiful.'

'Not exactly a proposal of marriage, that.' He gave a short laugh.

She was grateful for the darkness hiding the flame in her cheeks.

'I can't see your aunt agreeing,' he said. 'Nor your uncle, for that matter.'

She took a deep breath. 'I can make them. I will convince them.'

Patrick pressed his lips against her forehead and the sweet pungency of the punch filled her nostrils. 'And your parents?'

'Yes, and my parents, too.'

The atmosphere at Hastings Street was heavy with tension. At breakfast, Aunt Piggott had become irate on hearing her husband's account of Mr Martin's engagement to Caroline Walker. She was taking the rapid transfer of Mr Martin's affections personally. Not only did she suspend her remonstrations at Henrietta's failure to recognise her opportunity, but she had gone so far as to suggest Henrietta ride her own horse along The Course later that day.

Unfortunately, this degree of sympathy had the consequence of prompting her aunt to keep up a ceaseless stream of indignant chatter on the topic when all Henrietta wanted to do was lose herself in her piano practice. Henrietta was trying not to think about Patrick who was sequestered with Uncle Piggott with the intention of making his proposal.

'I've spoken with your uncle about Griffith,' continued Aunt Piggott. 'And he agrees with me that it's a waste to leave him in the Navy when he could be so useful to the agency on our own ships.'

'That's wonderful to hear, Aunt.'

This was one interruption that was welcome. Perhaps Uncle Piggott's beneficence might extend to her plight.

'Yes, indeed. I was glad to have thought of it.' Aunt Piggott paused as one of the servants bowed his way into the room. 'Yes?' she said impatiently.

'If you please, ma'am, Mr Piggott would like to speak with Miss Burbridge in his study.'

'Whatever for?' Aunt Piggott's question was for Henrietta, not the servant. 'I hope we are not to hear any more of Mr Martin. Well, well, off you go then.'

Henrietta followed the servant through the maze of stairs and hallways. Her mind whirred and she barely knew where she was.

Patrick was leaving as she entered. She searched his face for some indication of how the matter had gone but, apart from a single intense look, he gave no sign.

'Sit down, m'dear. Take the weight off.' Uncle Piggott smiled tiredly. 'Not that you have any weight to trouble your young feet, of course.'

It was only when she had taken her seat that his face became serious.

'I take it that you are aware of Patrick's proposal?'

'Yes, and—'

'And, I gather, you are sympathetic to the notion?

'Yes, and—'

'Now, now, first things first. Marriage is a serious business—a most serious business. Not to be taken on without full possession of the facts.'

'I know that—'

'You know, of course, that Patrick can bring nothing—nothing, you hear—to a marriage? You can't be affording pretty frocks and baubles and such on a clerk's salary, you know.'

'Yes, but Hastings himself started out as a writer's clerk, didn't he? And until Patrick establishes himself, my family—'

He held up a hand to quell her. 'It's an awkward business, my dear.' Uncle Piggott fiddled with the snuffbox on his desk and re-positioned the blotter. 'I'm not sure what your parents may have told you about dealings between us?' He took in her blank face. 'So, I'll assume that they have not told you. When they do, then it is likely their story will apportion blame entirely differently. However, I would like to tell you how I see it.' He cleared his throat and, his gaze fixed to the far wall, he began. 'When your grandmother passed on, she left her estate—consisting mainly of Barrow House—for the use of her second husband, Mr Andrews, during his lifetime.'

Henrietta remembered that her aunt had mentioned Barrow House as where the two half-sisters had finally lived as a family on their return from Calcutta.

'Following his death,' continued Uncle Piggott, more confidently, 'the estate was to be shared between your mother and your aunt. But when Mr Andrews died, it so happened that your father was selling his estates in preparation for the removal to New South Wales. I, that is, your aunt and I agreed to make an offer to buy out your mother's share of the house, rather than sell Barrow House outright at a time when the market prices were depressed. Your parents accepted the offer.'

Uncle Piggott's tone was no longer tinged with indulgent patronage. He spoke to her as an adult. 'Well, it turned out that the situation in New South Wales was not as rosy as painted by Sir Joseph Banks. Your father—well, your parents, as this concerns your mother too—have had occasion to regret the price they accepted for your mother's share of the estate. And, well, they have sought redress. They consider that we should pay them the difference between what they paid and the higher price we obtained when we later sold the estate. Naturally, we have refused.' He mopped his brow with his handkerchief. 'So when your mother wrote to suggest we might have you to stay, well, we thought, if we could assist in any way—without any imputation that the original transaction was in any way untoward, of course—well, we would.' He finished with a sigh of relief at having told the tale.

Henrietta had never heard Uncle Piggott speak for so long. She had come to appreciate that his joviality masked his sound acumen, which she witnessed when she accompanied him going about his agency business; however, in his interactions with traders, he said little and listened much. She thought over what he had said.

Everything accorded with what she knew of her father's disappointments and struggles. And, too, his formulation of resentments for past decisions aligned with what she understood of her father's character. She felt a flash of impatience. She wasn't to blame for Papa's poor financial decisions. Why should she be chastised for imprudence, when his mismanagement— and Mama's acquiescence—had placed her in this intolerable situation of dependency?

Uncle Piggott slumped back in his chair, and Henrietta's mood softened.

'Thank you for telling me, Uncle Piggott,' she said. 'I can see that you have tried your best to put matters clearly for me, and in a way that does no injury to any party.'

Uncle Piggott gave a small smile.

'And, of course, I am mindful of the need to be settled in suitable circumstances.' The image of Mr Martin floated into her mind, and something like regret began to nibble at the edges. She set her jaw. 'But, I'm afraid, I still don't understand how this would affect your decision as my guardian here in Calcutta regarding Patrick's proposal.'

Uncle Piggott looked miserable. 'I'll put it plain then, m'dear. Your parents are not in a position to release any funds for a dowry and, while I'm your guardian here in Calcutta, I'm still constrained by their wishes, of course. They'll not be agreeing, I'm afraid, and it would be wrong of me to be giving you or Patrick hope when none is possible.'

The weight of his words pressed down upon her.

He attempted another smile. 'And, after all, you're young. Things will change. If there's one thing I've learnt in business, my dear, is that things will change. You'll go back to Botany Bay—a glorious rose among the thorns. And your father's business will prosper, and you will have your pick of any of the suitors who'll come calling, you'll see. After all, you're only sixteen— there's no need to hurry.' He paused as though suddenly struck by a thought. 'There is no hurry, is there?' He fixed her with a look of worry.

Henrietta had stopped listening at the words 'back to Botany Bay'. And, she thought, *back to the Mr Babcocks of that thorny world.*

She retired early to bed that night. Her aunt's flood of goodwill had been staunched once she learnt from Uncle Piggott of Patrick's proposal. Aunt Piggott made it perfectly clear that she thought the whole matter preposterous and laid the blame squarely upon Henrietta, declaring that Patrick wouldn't have the wit or presumption to have thought of the idea himself.

Lakshmi laid out the pack of cards hopefully.

'Not now.' Henrietta flopped on the bed. At Lakshmi's look of disappointment, Henrietta added,

'I've taught you far too well. I can't concentrate on a thing and you'll win.'

Lakshmi took up her post outside the door, leaving Henrietta free to stare at the ceiling. The ceiling provided no answers. Aunt Piggott had decreed that Henrietta would return home on Griffith's first voyage on one of their uncle's ships headed for Sydney. It would sail in June—three months away. She'd be home in time for Eliza's marriage to Dr Forster, she thought dully.

If only Patrick had some money, or even expectations of money, or a title, or something that she could use to convince her parents to consent. The only thing to which she could cling was that Uncle Piggott seemed sympathetic—not that he had said this in so many words, but everything in his manner and his careful discussion of the sensitive family dealings gave that impression. Her examination of the ceiling steadily shrank to focus on a small gecko. It would dart a few steps then freeze, only to dart again. Each time it froze, she found herself holding her breath, waiting for its next movement for release.

A murmur of voices outside the door distracted her. The door slid open a chink and Patrick slid into the room.

'What are you doing?' Henrietta questioned.

'Coming to see you, of course. We have to talk.'

'But, Lakshmi …' Henrietta sprang from the bed.

'I'm a few paisas poorer, but she is now blind and deaf, in so far as we're concerned.'

Henrietta privately thought the money a poor investment, since Lakshmi's mother was Aunt Piggott's maidservant. However, there were more pressing matters.

'I couldn't persuade him,' she said.

'Nor I. But when we talked, there was one minute when he seemed almost amused. After all, "she's a bonnie lass".' He quoted Uncle Piggott. He then reached out to tuck a stray curl behind her ear. 'And "a man has to aim high in the world". And then the next minute, he'd break off muttering about family troubles, or some such.'

Henrietta took a couple of steps back out of arm's reach. 'It's just some business dispute. It shouldn't be the issue at all.' She sighed. 'But Papa will make it so.'

'What about your mother? Does she have any influence on your father?'

'Sometimes.' Henrietta was still trying to take in Uncle Piggotts' comment that it had been her mother who had sought the invitation for Henrietta to join the Piggotts in Calcutta.

'Which reminds me, your aunt tells me she's convinced Mr Piggott to pay Griffith out of the Navy.'

Henrietta permitted herself a smug smile.

'You're going to make somebody a formidable wife.' Patrick moved closer again, grasping her hand and pulling it to his lips. 'I wish it could be me.'

Henrietta drew her hand away. 'I'd take that as a compliment if you weren't taking so many liberties in the delivery.'

Patrick chuckled. 'Your uncle intimated some concern that I'd already taken more than my share.'

His words brought back Uncle Piggott's final question to her. 'The poor dear asked me something of the sort,' she said, suppressing a giggle.

'It does rather raise the question as to what mischief your uncle and aunt got up to themselves in their salad days, doesn't it?'

They both laughed then, caught by the ludicrousness of the thought.

'Sh, sh,' Henrietta whispered. 'Not so loud.'

Footsteps approached outside the door.

Patrick sprang back and moved rapidly through the curtains onto the verandah. By the speed with which he moved, it was clear he'd been in similar situations before.

At that moment, the door opened, and Aunt Piggott appeared, her maidservant by her side. Lakshmi stood behind them, her head low.

Aunt Piggott looked around the room, her eyes searching every crevice. Finally, she said in a controlled tone, 'Lakshmi can bring supper to your room, Henrietta.'

Henrietta waited for her to leave.

She wondered what the consequences would have been if Patrick had been found. An idea began to form in her mind.

The sunsets of that year had been the talking point of Calcutta. Lakshmi had assured her that the goddess Kali was angry, but the Dutch sea captains had brought back news of a volcanic eruption from Java, so massive that its cloud of ash slowly infiltrated the skies of the whole world. Tonight, as the sun paused, low on the horizon, the red-gold light shimmered across the water of the Hugli.

From their little boat, Henrietta felt she would only need to lean over the side to be able to scoop up handfuls of liquid fire and let it trickle through her fingers.

'Are you having second thoughts?' asked Patrick.

His back was to the sun, so she could only see his black shape seated by the rudder—she couldn't make out his expression.

'No, not at all.' The quaver in her voice betrayed her. 'It's the only way.' She went back over the plan in her mind.

They had repeated their ploy to spirit Henrietta away while she was ostensibly at her dance lessons. They planned to stay away from the house just long enough to raise the concern that they had eloped, but not so long that, once they returned, Henrietta's reputation would be jeopardised—around midnight should be sufficient.

'And you trust Lakshmi?' Patrick asked yet again.

'She knows what to say.'

And what not to say, Henrietta hoped. Henrietta had not told her where they intended to go—she didn't want to be pursued and brought back. That would only prompt her being sent home even earlier than planned in order to remove her from moral danger.

The river had been the only place she could think of where they'd be relatively safe from prying eyes. While she wanted her uncle and aunt to fear for her reputation, she didn't want to actually ruin it. Caroline's place couldn't be considered, of course, and the sorts of places which Patrick suggested would raise more questions about her virtue than was advisable. The river was busy, day or night, but not with the sort of people from their own social world who might set off the alarm. Only the Piggotts needed to know—that would be all that would be needed to convince them. It would be all right, she told herself. It was a good plan.

Neither Henrietta nor Patrick talked much as the sky purpled to the blue-black ink. The light breeze fell and Patrick steered close by the bank, securing the pinnace with a light anchor. Small cook fires glowed through the trees, and the sounds of distant chatter filtered across the water. The moon rose, blood-red. Slowly, the night became still and silent.

Henrietta shivered. She'd been sitting in the same cramped position and the damp air had seeped through her shawl.

Patrick cleared his throat. 'A drink would surely help about now.'

'Is it time?' she asked.

'Near enough, by my reckoning.'

Since there was no wind, Patrick rowed slowly back down the river, moving with the flow. He kept the pinnace close into shore, avoiding the possibility of running into the anchor chains of the large vessels in the main channel in the darkness.

Henrietta's fingers tightened into a fist as they came closer to the town. She pictured them walking into Hastings Street—Aunt Piggott berating them, or perhaps just berating her, while Patrick was taken to task by Uncle Piggott. Or would Lakshmi succumb to interrogation? Perhaps they'd find Uncle Piggott waiting for them at Chandpal Ghat or about to set off in pursuit?

As they rounded the last bend, a blaze of light flooded across the river from Fort William. Carrying clearly across the water came the stirring blast of horns signalling the finale of a military tune.

'What?' Patrick gaped.

Henrietta groaned. 'The military band. The concert's tonight. I forgot.'

'You forgot?' Patrick began trying to row back against the current, trying to manoeuvre the pinnace out of the light.

'So did you,' she retorted. She felt sick with fear. She'd been so wrapped up in her scheming, she'd completely forgotten about the performance.

Despite Patrick's efforts, they drifted closer and closer. They could see more clearly the figures of people starting to make their way past the Water Gate and along the promenade that ran alongside the bank, back towards the town.

They'd be seen. She looked to Patrick. The current was too strong. They were drifting with the current to where the light melded into the river like molten wax. He shook his head in defeat and raised the oars out of the water.

They were close enough now for her to recognise two of the figures closest to the water's edge—Sir James Caldwell was pointing something out in the night sky to Lady Caldwell and Miss Prendergast. Their gaze followed his pointing finger, but if they looked down, then there was nowhere for Henrietta or Patrick to hide.

'Row,' she demanded.

Patrick gave a start and dipped the oars, ready for one last effort.

It was too late.

Miss Prendergast's mouth popped open and she grasped Lady Caldwell's arm. Henrietta watched with dread as Lady Caldwell's head turned, slowly, inexorably, towards where Patrick and she sat, marooned in a pool of light. For a brief hysterical moment, Henrietta thought to raise her hand in greeting, but she stayed motionless until at last the current moved them past and into the protection of the night.

'No, no, no,' she whispered, her face in her hands.

'Perhaps they won't—'

'They will.'

Chapter 14

The truth

Reverend Bryce paced the floor once more. He seemed to be deciding how best to begin.

'Your aunt is worried about you, Henrietta.'

His words hung in the air between them. Henrietta sat, head bowed, not daring to meet Reverend Bryce's eye. The Reverend was Aunt Piggott's idea, of course. Her aunt's efforts had failed to elicit a guilty plea from either Henrietta or Patrick. Uncle Piggott had taken refuge alone in his study, pleading pressure of business. Reverend Bryce, being Presbyterian, wasn't Henrietta's minister, but Aunt Piggott had little confidence in the Anglican chaplain and, given the delicacy of the matter, she was reluctant to go directly to Bishop Middleton for fear of giving weight to rumour.

'So I am aware,' Henrietta replied. She had listened to her aunt's concerns for three days. She was exhausted. She couldn't sleep. When she did drift off, the memory of her aunt's tirade would shake her back into wakefulness.

'Your aunt only wants to assess the situation. You must understand that she needs to write to your parents. If you were to arrive back in Sydney in, shall we say, a compromised state, then there would be serious consequences indeed, and not solely for yourself.'

Henrietta thought uncomfortably back to the conversation she had had with Uncle Piggott regarding the strain between the two families.

'I can assure you, Reverend Bryce, that I am not compromised, as you put it. I have told my aunt as much, but she refuses to believe me.' Her eyes were gritty with lack of sleep and she couldn't see the difficulty. 'Patrick and I wish to marry. We considered elopement but, mindful of the worry to our aunt and uncle, we did not. Surely, you cannot think us wrong to wish to marry with their permission?'

Reverend Bryce stopped his pacing and gave her a shrewd look. 'No longer the blushing young gel I introduced to the governor-general, I see. You have grown up quickly in Calcutta, Miss Burbridge.'

She looked at him directly for the first time but held her tongue.

'You are looking tired, my dear,' he said. With a look of resignation, he added, 'Your aunt will be expecting to have a word with me before I take my leave. Might I suggest you retire to your room to rest. It might be your last chance for a while, one way or another.'

Henrietta followed his advice, though without any confidence that sleep would be possible. It was dark when she opened her eyes. Lakshmi was leaning over her.

'Miss Burbridge, you have a visitor.'

Lakshmi's worried face was replaced by another. Patrick was bent so close to her that she could feel his soft breath on her cheeks.

'We've done it, Henrietta, we've done it.'

'We have? What?' She sat bolt upright, bumping into Patrick's forehead.

He jumped back. 'Careful there, take care with your future husband. You don't want to break the merchandise before you've paid for it.'

'But, but what are you doing in here?' Still trying to shake off sleep, she couldn't take in what he was saying. 'We're in enough trouble as it is without you getting caught in my room again. What if Lakshmi—'

'We have Lakshmi to thank,' he said, sitting on the edge of the bed.

'How?' she asked, wriggling into a sitting position, drawing her legs up away from him. He was too close for comfort.

'Just when your aunt was beginning to believe that nothing untoward occurred, Lakshmi let slip about our previous boating excursion on the Hugli.'

'But that was just so I could see Griffith,' Henrietta protested.

'Ah, but Lakshmi didn't know that, did she? All she knew was that we had been gone a very long time.'

Henrietta stared at him. His eyes were flashing with mischief. She couldn't help but be drawn in.

'I suppose we could tell them the truth,' she said, eyebrows raised.

'Perhaps,' he smiled. He drew her hand into his. 'But why let truth get in the way of a happy ending? Lakshmi's story was enough to convince your aunt that nothing should delay our nuptials. She's got Uncle Piggott writing to tell your parents that they wholeheartedly approve the match, particularly as ...' He paused for effect. 'I am to be made a partner of Piggott, Davidson and Robertson.'

The wedding was smaller than she would have liked but, as Aunt Piggott managed to remind her at every opportunity, it was for the best, *given the circumstances*. Henrietta was not able to disabuse her aunt of the need for speed, as to do so would undermine the grounds upon which permission had been granted.

St John's Church was located behind her uncle's property in Hastings Street, and it was decided that their little party would walk there as, despite the summer heat, the morning air stirred with a slight breeze. Uncle Piggott had dressed in his finest brocaded waistcoat and had gone so far as to purchase new shoes for the occasion. Aunt Piggott insisted that her maidservant hold a parasol above her head to protect her complexion, though she was heard to comment that the weather was 'nearly as pleasant as England', so Henrietta took this to mean that she was enjoying herself enormously. Uncle Piggott had co-opted the ever-obliging Commodore John Hayes as a witness, under the inducement of joining the family at the wedding breakfast to follow.

It was cooler inside the church, and the skin on Henrietta's arms prickled. All the planning and scheming that she had done to reach India, to escape the prospect of Mr Martin, and to find a way to avoid returning home—it had all brought her to this moment. She'd barely had time for thought since the wheels had been put in motion. There was the short time before the wedding; not to mention organising the ceremony, writing letters home, visiting the small apartments that Uncle Piggott had built for them above the new *godown* in Shibpur, and making plans with Patrick for their honeymoon sailing further up the Hugli—all the rush had come to this moment.

Time stopped, as if pausing to take a breath.

Through that small, still space, Uncle Piggott took her to where Patrick stood, waiting, his face solemn. She took her place beside him and time began again.

Reverend Shephard moved them through the ceremony at a pace that suggested he was more than ready for the wedding breakfast. The curate struggled under the weight of the Register. Once open, its pages were so long and wide that Henrietta couldn't have reached across. Now that the ceremony was over, the onlookers were chattering. Henrietta signed where Reverend Shephard indicated. She watched as Patrick inscribed his name.

'Alexander Norton Richeley?' she asked. 'Richeley? Did I not know whom I was marrying?'

'Uncle Piggott insisted on a new name for me— seemed to think it was fitting,' he said with a wry smile.

So the toasts at the wedding breakfast back at Hastings Street were all to *Mr and Mrs Richeley*. Henrietta reflected on the power wielded by whoever held the pocketbook. But with each toast, her disquiet dissipated. She even began to find Aunt Piggott amusing as she listened to her lengthy description of her own wedding, against the backdrop of Patrick's *sotto voce* innuendo. Aunt Piggott had made certain to invite Lady Caldwell and Miss Prendergast.

'He isn't wearing his slippers, surely?' whispered Miss Prendergast, eyeing Uncle Piggott's feet.

As usual, he'd swapped his shoes for his oriental footwear as soon as he'd arrived home.

Lady Caldwell raised her eyebrows in abhorrence.

'I see that Mr Martin has not been invited,' she said, ostensibly to Miss Prendergast, but her voice cut through the surrounding conversational babble. 'I may not look it, but I'm old enough to remember how it was when he was just a young man and courting our dear Mrs Piggott-to-be.' She tsked and turned her head from the looks of inquiry from some of the women standing nearby. 'Such gossips, people are.'

Miss Prendergast added, 'And Miss Walker couldn't make it, I see.'

Henrietta was not sorry to avoid the social navigation that the presence of the affianced couple would have involved. However, she was sorry that it was not possible to invite Babu Dutt. Uncle Piggott assured her that Babu Dutt wouldn't be expecting an invitation, but Henrietta thought that it would have been courteous at the very least to return the favour of his invitation to his daughter's wedding.

She was enjoying listening as Reverend Bryce needled Reverend Shephard about the paltry spire that graced St John's, when Patrick pulled her to one side.

'How soon do you think we might be excused from the company, Mrs Richeley?' There was a slight indistinctness about his speech that mirrored his enthusiastic participation in the toasts.

'Why, Mr Richeley, how scandalous do you think we should be?' she countered. In truth, she was not feeling scandalous in the least. She felt very young, all of a sudden. She wished there were a few more toasts so that she might feel less so.

'A song,' cried Uncle Piggott. 'We shall have a song from the lovely couple.'

Henrietta played the accompaniment as Patrick sang, his hand resting on the pianoforte to steady himself. His rich voice slipped through her body like warm chocolate. It would all be all right. It had to be. She watched Uncle Hogue's beaming face and wondered what advice he would give her—'it's a foreign country, m'dear, but you'll get used to it, you'll soon get used to it'.

THE END

Author's note

I have drawn heavily from available historical records to paint a picture of the lives of the main characters in this novel. I have fictionalised the names of the main characters because I cannot know their personal feelings and motivations, and so the novel's plot, events and themes are my own invention. Thus, the Burbridge families and their relatives by birth or marriage are fictional characters, inspired by the family of Mr John Blaxland (older brother to the explorer, Gregory Blaxland). However, I have retained the names of well-known historical figures who appear or who are referred to in the novel, and for whom considerable material is available upon which to ground their depiction.

One of the greatest areas of difficulty in writing this novel was in reconciling the views of the historical characters about race and class with contemporary cultural awareness.

In the early 1800s, the era in which the novel is set, Sydney was a small settlement of about 30,000 people, about two-thirds of whom were convicts or ex-convicts, with the convict population almost at its peak. The population was rapidly growing, so social connections were continually changing and adjusting. The historical characters of this novel lived among a small elite (the 'exclusives') within a penal colony, where the main source of labour for their homes and estates was provided by convicts, convicts' children, and convicts who had served their time ('emancipists').

The settlement sat at the edge of a large continent populated by multiple Aboriginal tribes whose clan groups were being progressively dispossessed with the uptake of land as the colony grew. The attitudes described in this novel were based on family records and were typical of their class. Awareness of Aboriginal people was strikingly absent in the records which inspired my depiction of the women in the Burbridge family.

One of the key sources for the novel was the memoir of Lady Harriet Dowling (born Blaxland, formerly Richie), in which she recorded her impressions of wealthy Indians, as well as her observations of servants and people in their everyday practices, yet she made no mention of Aboriginal people in New South Wales.

The Blaxlands' involvement in the events that preceded and followed the removal of Governor Bligh from office occurred as described.

While it is possible to glean something of Harriet's life and character from her memoir and from the accounts of others, relatively little is known about childhood of the many Blaxland children (though more is known about their later lives). For this reason, I have portrayed their characters based on my speculation as to their lives as children.

For a detailed bibliography of sources and a longer factual account of the events and people who inspired this work of fiction, readers may be interested in the short biography I have written previously on the life of Harriet Blaxland.

A Ferguson, *A gentleman's daughter: The life of Harriet Mary Dowling (nee Blaxland) in India and Australia in colonial times*, Backstory Press, New South Wales, 2017.

(available in e-book or paperback via Amazon)

Acknowledgements

My husband, Ian King, gets top billing in my list of 'thankyou's. Without his detailed background knowledge of the Blaxland history and his constant support and encouragement, this project would have stalled a long time ago. My thanks are also owed to Richard Blaxland and Wendy Blaxland for their enthusiastic support. I am very appreciative of the librarians at the State Library of New South Wales for enabling my access to their collection which includes materials related to the Blaxland, Dowling and Walker families.

My thanks to the members of the Lake Macquarie branch of the Fellowship of Australian Writing for their support and invaluable feedback in the development of this novel and my other writing over many years. Thanks also to my trusty beta-readers—Jenny Ferneyhough, Sue McAllister, and Glenys Murray—for their insightful comments and suggestions on this story and all the others. And finally, thanks too for the polish to the final product from the detailed editing provided courtesy of the Manuscript Appraisal Agency, Katoomba, New South Wales. Any remaining glitches remain, of course, my own.

About the author

After completing a degree in writing in the early 70s, my interest in communication led me to qualify and work as a speech pathologist in clinical and academic settings. Now retired, I am pursuing my long-standing fascination with story writing across diverse genres.

In 2017, I self-published 'A Gentleman's Daughter'—a biography of Harriet Blaxland (later, Lady Dowling) who lived a colourful life in colonial New South Wales and India (available in paperback and eBook through Amazon and other online retailers). Over the last few years, I have written a number of award-winning short stories ranging across crime, horror, and historical science fiction. My unpublished science-fiction novel 'Grey Nomad' was shortlisted for the 2019 Fantastic Prize (Brio Books), the Queensland Writers' Centre 2020 Adaptable and Publishable programs, and I currently have a crime novel 'in the works'.

Next in the trilogy

Volume 2

in The Sisters' Saga

Dearest Daughter is the second of three in *The Sisters' Saga*, which tells of three sisters and the compromises they must make to reconcile love's delusions with the demands of reality.

In this short historical fiction novel, the lives of the younger sisters, Rose and Beth Burbridge are turned upside down by Henrietta's return from India.

In colonial Sydney between 1825-35, Henrietta asks why, if matrimony is the bedrock of the families, is it so hard for love to survive marriage?

But her sisters must answer a very different question: How much would they trade for matrimony?